IF SHE PLAYS HIS GAME

After Twelve Series, Book Two

Laney Wylde

THIS BOOK is a work of fiction. Names, characters, places and incidents are the product of the author's imagination or are used fictitiously. Any resemblance to actual persons, living or dead, business establishments, events or locales is entirely coincidental.

NO PART of this book may be reproduced, scanned, or distributed in any printed or electronic form without permission. Please do not participate in or encourage piracy of copyrighted materials in violation of the author's rights. Purchase only authorized editions.

IF SHE PLAYS HIS GAME
Copyright ©2018 Laney Wylde
All rights reserved.
Printed in the United States of America
First Print Edition: May 2019

WWW.CRIMSONTREEPUBLISHING.COM

SUMMARY: Estlyn is good at cutting deals. The one she's working on now will get her a clean criminal record—and get her brother and incarcerated father off the hook, too. The problem is, she's going to have to orchestrate a murder to get it done. It's a conscience-wrenching assignment. To make matters worse, she'll have to reach out to a contact from her past—one she'd hoped to never see again.

ISBN: 978-1-63422-341-6 (paperback)
ISBN: 978-1-63422-340-9 (e-book)
Cover Design by: Marya Heidel
Typography by: Courtney Knight
Editing by: Cynthia Shepp

Fiction / Romance / New Adult
Fiction / Thrillers / Legal
Fiction / Romance / Multicultural & Interracial
Fiction / Romance / Contemporary

For Stacey.
Without your persistent affirmation combating my self-doubt,
this book and all my others would not exist.
I will forward all complaints your way.

She may be going to Hell, of course, but at least she isn't standing still.

~E. E. Cummings

ONE

Estlyn

Sixteen Days Prior

I'M NOT GOOD AT poker because I can lie. I'm good at poker because I know who else does. That's how I'm certain DA Gavin Young is full of bullshit.

His tone is as casual as his parting hands when he says, "What we're looking for is a one-time campaign cataclysm—something Sellards won't recover from." He rocks back in his leather desk chair, which I can only assume was made from cows he himself slaughtered. "We want, if you will, to Willie Horton his Dukakis."

Okay, that's not the bullshit part. Young has never been more genuine, which is why when he said that he wants a Willie Horton, I heard, *Knock my shiny capped teeth out*. But I won't. I'm not violent.

MLK, bitches.

I drop my hands to my lap to keep my balled fists from showing and take a calming breath to slow the blood boiling to my face. This, I doubt, is what my doctor had in mind when she said four stress-free weeks. I mean, contempt and dread aren't exactly yoga.

For those unfamiliar with 1980's politics or the proper noun Young coerced into a verb, allow me to translate: *What we're looking for is a batshit-crazy murderer tethered to Sellards's campaign like an anchor that will drag him down in a sea of Young votes until his chances at governor drown.* That's what convicted murderer Willie Horton did for George H. W. Bush's campaign when he raped a woman and killed both her and her husband during one of his regular weekends off from his Massachusetts prison. Michael Dukakis was the governor of Massachusetts at the time and supported letting violent criminals roam free on Saturdays and Sundays for church or synagogue or a little homicide and sexual assault. Bush, of course, blamed Dukakis for Horton's actions. Much of the country did the same after they saw the picture of the deranged killer Dukakis had unleashed on his constituents every week. The resulting 1988 presidential election was no contest.

Oh, and Willie Horton happened to be black.

"As you know," Young continues, "in this political climate, it's going to be difficult, if not impossible, for me to win without a Willie Horton."

Oh please, continue to bring up the erroneous

symbol of black violence. It's not like I have a dad locked in prison because of the perpetuation of that stereotype.

"You may already know that Sellards is a partner in a pro bono law firm that ferociously defends drug offenders in Los Angeles. He specializes in helping those who already have strikes on their records," he scoffs. "My interns have combed through all of his cases to find an acquittal-turned-violent crime."

I raise an eyebrow. "Have they had any luck?"

He sighs. "Not yet. That's where you come in."

"Excuse me?"

"Well..." He smiles against the fingertips pressed together at his lips. "You're an expert at framing people, aren't you?"

I put my hands on his desk and straighten in my chair. "Sir, I think you have a gross misunderstanding of what I do. I do not *frame* people for a living." Massaging my forehead, I answer, "I simply create opportunities for people to incriminate themselves."

"Oh, you didn't frame Officer Monroe?"

My arms cross over my chest. "After Twelve didn't. *I* did."

"Well, if it makes you sleep better at night, *you're going to create an opportunity* for someone to incriminate himself for a heinous crime."

"You're asking me to put an innocent man behind bars for life."

"Ms. Collins," he condescends, "we aren't talking about some upstanding citizen. We're talking about a convicted felon. A thug. A lowlife. No matter who he is, he should be locked up anyway."

I sigh back into my chair. "What kind of crime?"

"Something Willie Horton disastrous."

I wonder if those caps would fall off his shaved-to-points front teeth if I hit him hard enough. I wonder if I'll find out if he says *Willie Horton* one more time. Because I'm not Martin Luther King, Jr. I'll never have that commanding voice or courage or effortless sexual magnetism.

"Just to confirm," I sit up to say, "you want the equivalent of two dead bodies and a bloody crime scene for the six o'clock news." My finger coils through the air when I add, "Then you want to turn that into an attack ad that says…" Dropping my voice to a menacing baritone, I continue. "Sellards aggressively defended this murderer. These two people would be alive and well if it weren't for him. Vote for Young. Tough on Crime."

He nods and flashes that overpriced smile. "Exactly. Sellards supports repealing the third-strike law altogether, so getting someone who should be in prison for life on their third strike if he hadn't gotten them off would be ideal."

I exhale a reluctant, "Got it. You have anyone

in mind?"

"Emmy has a box of case files on would-be third strikers who were acquitted with Sellards as their attorney. I trust you can choose the convict and crime that will work best in our time frame. We need this to happen within the next month."

Right, I will find the life most convenient for me to ruin.

I nod and stand to leave. Young reaches his hand out, and I force mine to take his.

"Remember, it's one thug in prison in exchange for you, Rory, and your dad. Better him than you, right?"

Ah, spoken like a true prosecutor. There are no souls, just bargaining chips.

With a strangled breath, I nod.

TWO

Estlyn

Fifteen Days Prior

DEAN SURRENDERED ALL MY devices to the police the night they raided my apartment, but I left Young's office yesterday with my laptop, tablet, and chargers—all packed in plastic evidence bags. *Suck it, Dean.* Four weeks of medical leave my gorgeous, round ass.

At my dining table, I kick my feet up on the opposite chair and log into my email. After some serious persuading, which involved a list of bills he would have to pay if I didn't work, Rory got my access back. And holy shit there are a ton of requests in my inbox. All I need right now is a paycheck. Something quick, high paying, low profile—likely a cheating case from an upper-class, soon-to-be divorcée. I sift through the subject lines.

Student Framed Me for Affair with Her. I'm sure she did.

Priceless Painting Stolen. That sounds tedious.

That's what private investigators are for. I open the email to find an offer of $250,000 to retrieve the painting and *adequately punish the thieves*. My lord, is this a Dali? Who has that kind of money to ransom a painting? Fine, if I stumble upon a museum-worthy canvas not in a museum, I'll toss it in the trunk of my car.

Neighbor Poisoned My Cat. Well, that's hard to prove. And did the dander-laden jerk shit in her yard? Did he scratch her toddler? I mean, did he have it coming? I only take cases where I'm convinced my client deserves the justice they're asking for. I'm afraid I have yet to be able to prove a cat's innocence beyond a reasonable doubt. Those little bastards are hard to read. I mean, what the hell is with those creepy-ass vertical irises?

Husband Cheating with Coworker. Ding, ding, ding! A winner. I love me a vindictive housewife. They're angry and desperate and eager to spend money from a joint checking account. Their story is always some version of the following:

> *Boy meets girl.*
> *Boy marries girl.*
> *Boy inserts babies in girl.*
> *Girl gets squishy and stretched out.*
> *Boy advances in his career.*
> *Girl's respect for boy does not advance to his liking.*

IF SHE PLAYS HIS GAME

Boy meets younger girl who he says respects him but actually just makes him hard.
Boy butt-dials girl during intercourse with younger girl.
Girl packs up boy's kids in minivan to leave.
Girl decides boy should leave instead and unpacks said van.
Girl decides boy should hurt as much as she does.
Girl contemplates plan involving Sweeney Todd
scissors to boy's groin.
Girl gets my card from friend whose boy I made
hurt.
Girl abandons Sweeney-esqe scheme and pays me to hurt boy.
In this case, the girl is Emory Rush, and her message to me is textbook.

Samson,
I recently discovered that my husband of eleven years has been having an affair. He is a vascular surgeon at UCLA Medical Center and is sleeping with a resident. I'm not sure how long it has been going on, but last month I found a thong in the bag he takes to work. After that, I noticed a phone number he texts more frequently than any other on our cell bill. When he was asleep, I read the texts from her. See the attached photo for evidence.

She sent me a porn photo of her husband's mistress? I peek at the thumbnail attachment. Yep, she did. And I can't unsee it.

Please help me leave my husband with some of my dignity intact. I'm available to meet any morning during the week while my kids are in school.
Sincerely,

Emory Rush

My reply is brief.

Emory,
My assis
tant will meet with you tomorrow at Philz Coffee in Santa Monica at 9:00.
Please bring a 50% deposit of $10,000 along with all pertinent information about your husband and his mistress. If you have a prenuptial agreement, please bring a copy.
We look forward to the opportunity to work with you.
Justice always,

Samson

I shut my laptop and rest my shoulders against the back of the chair. My heart attack vacation is officially over.

THREE

Cal

Fifteen Days Prior

"**Whitney is ready for** you," my agent's assistant announces with no more than a glance in my direction. I stand and sling my bag over my shoulder, then head toward the closed door with *Whitney Kilberg* on it.

Today is the first day I've looked forward to in this entire shitty week. Whitney, the agent Estlyn connected me with, might already have a buyer for my script. I'm focusing on that—on the possibility of no longer sleeping on Elliot's couch, on the one good thing that came out of my "relationship" with Estlyn—instead of the fact that she hasn't reached out to me since I left her passed out in her bed, or that I'm worried she had another heart attack and died there alone. Because it's not my problem. She was just using me. So now I'm going to take advantage of what I can still get from her.

Stiletto heels on the desk greet me when I

push open Whitney's door. My eyes journey up the long legs they're attached to until I see delicate fingers holding my script. Behind the pages is a familiar face in glasses.

Manipulative bitch.

No, that isn't the first thought that pops in my mind when I see Estlyn on the other side of that desk. My initial thought is, *She's alive! She's okay! Why isn't she home resting?* And instead of being pissed like a normal human, I'm stoked to see her.

People as dumb as me deserve to be screwed over by people as cunning as Estlyn.

"Have a seat, Linus," she says without looking up from the script.

I should turn on my heel and storm out, but I can't compel my feet to the door. "Where's Whitney?"

Estlyn's dark eyes meet mine. "Vape break." Her attention returns to my screenplay as she flips the page. "I see that you used narration. Have you considered replacing that with asides?"

Asides? What the hell is she talking about? "Is there even a producer interested, or is this just another one of your elaborate lies?"

Estlyn gestures with her pen-wielding hand and continues, "Narration is tired." Then she quickly adds a reassuring, "not that I think your narration is a problem, per se. It adds a level of wit and, at some points, is even moving. But I don't want to just hear E. E. Cummings commentary. I want him melting me with those stormy blue eyes as he tells me about his deliciously depraved lust for his friend's wife."

I pound my hands against the desk, locking my elbows as I press my palms into the surface. "Is Whitney even my agent, or have I been emailing with you this whole time?"

Estlyn's feet gingerly kick off the desk, and she tosses her loose curls behind her shoulder. She turns the script to me and taps her pen on a passage of narration. "For instance, in this scene where he's with his friend after sleeping with his wife the night before, Cummings could speak this voice-over directly into the camera, *Big Short* style."

We stare at each other for several moments, each waiting for the other to engage in the conversations we're each persisting in.

"Are you not familiar with *The Big Short*? Have you seen *House of Cards*? That's another—"

"Estlyn," I say calmly, firmly. "Stop dicking around with my career. Do I have an agent or not?"

"Of course you do. She's on a vape break." Estlyn eyes me up and down. "You're welcome to take a seat, Linus."

"It's Cal," I correct, but I do sit down.

"Oh, right. I read something about that a few days ago." She scans the desk until she finds a sheet of lined yellow paper. From it, she reads the note I left her the afternoon I saw the article about her little revenge business.

"'Let them go—'" she reads. "'The truthful liars and the false fair friends and the boths and neithers—you must let them go they were born to go.' Hope your client is satisfied. –Cal."

She whips her glasses off and leans forward, pushing her breasts together like Erin Brockovich but without Erin Brockovich's tits. My eyes drift to her cleavage, but I lash them back to her face. "I deduce from this Cummings passage that I am the liar you are letting go. Of what lie am I guilty, Linus?"

Shit, she put the preposition at the beginning of the sentence. I hate that it makes me want to slip the next button of her shirt open. And the one below it. Damn it! I'm looking at her boobs again. *Eye contact.*

"It's Cal," I remind her.

She flicks her fingers in the air to dismiss my correction.

"You fucked me for your job. Which, by the way, is a downright disturbing profession. What is it you do, exactly? Do you go around cutting off fingers and dicks and then deliver them to your clients?"

Her voice is soft when she answers, but her volume doesn't diminish the conviction with which she speaks. "Linus, my job is neither violent nor illegal. All my targets sustain is professional and legal damage."

"Isn't extortion illegal?"

Her shoulders inch toward her ears. "How is extortion any different than threatening someone with a long prison sentence to get them to snitch or confess? This kind of bargaining, it's…" she scans the wall behind me, "…ethically grey. I doubt anyone could put me in jail for it."

Fine. I can understand that. Lawyers do all kinds of sleazy shit. It doesn't sound like she's worse than some scumbag attorney who keeps murderers out of prison.

I cross my arms. "You still fucked me for your job."

She squints and tilts her head. "Did I?"

"You picked me up at the bar because you knew I was Ron Calloway's son. Weren't you hired to ruin his reputation?"

Her hands meet at her chin as if in prayer. "Hmm." She turns, types into Whitney's computer, then turns the monitor to me. "As you may recall, you and I had our first sexual encounter on Tuesday, June fifth. Do you concur?"

Is this what it's like to be questioned by her on the witness stand? Is it wrong that I'm more aroused by her now than I was when she hit on me that first night? "Uh, yeah, that sounds right."

She points to the screen with the back of the pen. "Here, you will see the inquiry from a Ms.

Lola Sanchez. Can you read the time and date on this email for me?"

I sit up and shift my pants down my thighs just a smidge to make room for what should not be happening inside them. To answer my earlier question: yes, there is something wrong with me. "June sixth, 6:14 AM."

"This is the same Ms. Sanchez who, at one o'clock that same afternoon, asked me to get justice for her daughter, who'd been victimized by Taylor East, the star of your father's show. Mr. Calloway, do you agree I invited you to my apartment before I could have possibly had any professional motivation to?"

"I guess so."

"While I did, in fact, use your emergency contacts to reach out to your father and ex-girlfriend, do you see any association with you after the night of June sixth constituted a risk to my success in the Sanchez case? Isn't it true that, if you had found out before I secured justice for Mia, I would have failed at my job and sustained financial loss?"

"I think that's true."

"Furthermore, at any point after we met, did I overtly lie to you about my intentions for our relationship?"

"Um—"

Her volume rises, her tone growing stern. "Mr. Calloway, do you have any evidence to support your claim that I deceived you, that my actions did not match the nature of the relationship upon which we agreed? Or," she pushes off her chair to stand over me, "is it the truth that your accusations of deception are not only woefully inaccurate, but bordering libelous?"

I sit back in my chair with my clasped hands resting between my thighs. Her eyes are narrowed on mine, waiting for me to respond. Wow, I pissed her off. I might have even hurt her.

Does that mean she likes me?

Oh my God, Estlyn likes me. She didn't call or text to try to get me back; she took a few days to plot a way to stalk and corner me—a form of a flattery so pure, I'm not even creeped out. Or maybe I'm not creeped out because, as I've already established, there's something wrong with me. Probably a little of both.

I smirk. "Aren't you supposed to be resting at home?"

Her left eyebrow arches. "Aren't you supposed to be there making sure I am?" She scoops her bag off the floor and moves from behind the desk. "Think about those asides. You have a stellar story. They'll make it stand out from the slush pile."

I watch as she struts past me and closes the door behind her.

FOUR

Estlyn

FIFTEEN DAYS PRIOR

I DON'T NEED TO call him. That would mean I am desperate, that I've run out of alternatives. There are other options.

For instance, Rory and I could flee to a country with no extradition arrangement with the United States. I type a quick search for such nations on my laptop. The list isn't promising. Wait, I could live in Morocco. No, United Arab Emirates. I've heard they have some swanky shit there. That could be fun. Rory and Olivia could raise their baby in a glitzy high-rise with me living in an apartment down the hall. Liv would get on board eventually.

Probably.

Maybe.

But I'd never see my dad again.

Shit, I have to call him, don't I?

Maybe I could get Rory to take some kind of plea bargain that lowers his involvement to a misdemeanor. I'd pay his fine and do four years behind bars. I could handle prison. I'd just have to do those pushups Michael always nagged me about. I might even learn how to do a whole chin-up. Fuck, who am I kidding? Those bitches would snap me like a twig.

Crap. I'm calling him. Because if I don't find a not-Willie Horton to frame, who is Young going to murder, and whose DNA is he going plant at the scene?

"Quinton Cunningham's office," his assistant answers.

God, I forgot how douchey his name sounds out loud. I already regret this.

"Hi, this is Dillon Collins. Is Quinton available?"

"One moment."

Classy-ass hold music plays while I wait for her to inevitably return and say he's in a meeting. But it's just my luck that she doesn't.

"Cunningham," he answers.

I take a deep breath before I set the bridge to my escape on fire. "Hey Quin, it's Dillon Collins from—"

"Dil the dainty defender with a dick?" Alliteration used to be his favorite. While it doesn't add to his douchiness, it sure as hell makes me hate him more.

"Yeah." Sighing, I rub the back of my neck.

"To what do I owe the pleasure? Are you

ready to come over to the light side?"

God, prosecutors and their moral supremacy. "Are you?"

He cackles. "You haven't changed. I'm surprised you can sleep at night after *The People vs. Abigail O'Shea*."

I don't sleep, but not because the charges got dropped against some homicide suspect a few years ago. God, that trial lasted two eternities. That's how I met Quin, by the way. I was a second-year law student working on my professor's case, and Quin, who reeked of old money, was a recent grad working for the deputy district attorney. The story he sticks to is that he was smitten the moment he saw me taking notes on the opposite side of the courtroom. I was the Juliet to his Romeo—the bleeding-heart defense attorney's protégée, beautiful and forbidden by the age-old feud between the ruthless, justice-seeking prosecution and the defense, who had long since sold their souls at the rate of eight hundred dollars per billable hour.

The real story: he liked my ass in a pencil skirt. I'm not saying he was shallow—my ass looks scrumptious in a pencil skirt. And I'm sure Romeo's dick grew two sizes when he saw Juliet, too, but in that story, Juliet wasn't repulsed by both Romeo and his career dehumanizing alleged criminals.

Reducing lawbreakers to subhuman status

has been a prestigious path for Quin. He must be good at it because he's the youngest DDA in Los Angeles County history. Consequently, he's a regrettable necessity to survive my deal with DA Young.

"So, if this isn't a work call"—*for the record, I never said this wasn't a strictly professional conversation*—"has the official period of mourning ended? Am I finally allowed to ask you out for a drink?"

Wow, he *is* still an ass. *Yes, Quin, I've been waiting with bated breath until it was socially acceptable to go on a date with you after the brutal killing of my first and only love, who, by the way, your colleagues failed to obtain justice for. After five years, I'm totally over holding him as he bled out and can't wait to get in your pants. Please take me out for a drink!*

I want to give him one of those business cards Dean printed up for me years ago that say *Fuck off* on the front and *I'm mourning* on the back. Since Michael died, many men at bars, outside of court, and on the UCLA campus have received these. Also, this one bitch behind me in line at Express. As much as Quin deserves one now, I have to say, "A drink sounds great. Pick me up at eight at the apartments on Ocean Avenue."

"Perfect."

"Should I wear something nice, or does your government salary only pay you enough to take me to a dive?"

He snickers. "I'll be in the red Audi convertible."

I get it. You're rich.

"Aw, did Daddy buy that for you?" I tease. Shit, I should be more careful. I need to kiss his ass.

"My dad died in February."

Damn it! "Oh, Quin, I'm so—"

"I'm kidding! That son of a bitch will bury us all. See you at eight."

I throw my hands up and grit my teeth behind the veil of the phone. "Looking forward to it."

FIVE

Cal

Fifteen Days Prior

I LEAN ONTO THE bar and scroll through available apartments on my phone. The producer made me an offer of $175,000 against $350,000 for my script. Whitney wants to counter for $200,000 against $400,000. I think we should take what we can get so I can move the hell out of Elliot's.

When I returned from staying at Estlyn's, I was struck by the odor of his apartment. What had once been ignorable was now of unbearable potency. I spent an entire morning searching for the source without success. I fear now that the stench has infiltrated the drywall, carpet, and furniture. The only solution is to admit it is the greater adversary and retreat to a cleaner environment.

Then limit the time Elliot spends there.

A knock on the bar startles me. My attention moves to the familiar, tan hand on the counter. The third time today? Is everyone in Estlyn's circle conspiring against me? I shouldn't be flattered. I'm not.

Okay, I'm a little flattered.

Fine. The truth is, I've never had a girl chase me down before, and I'm relishing all five hours of it. Estlyn—who Elliot confirmed on multiple occasions is way out of my league—not only hit on me first but keeps coming back. That means I can do better than her. Or I should at least act that way until I have evidence to the contrary.

I push off the counter to stand up straight. "Estlyn's driving you to day drink?"

Dean sits on the stool in front of me and spreads his elbows to point in opposite directions. "No, she's not, actually. I think you broke her." As if he didn't just drop that anvil of guilt on me, he adds, "Whiskey, please."

I nod and reach for the bottle and a glass.

"I never shared the wisdom I promised you last week. Remember? That old gay hit on me, I had to pee, and then your ex interrupted us?"

"Yeah, somewhere between you telling me Estlyn was a toddler and a pathological liar, you took off."

He smiles as I pass him his drink. "You mean something to her."

"A connection for a case."

"Oh, lord, are you hung up on that? So she used you. So what? People use each other all the time. Even I used my ex to get out of a ticket."

"Okay, I'm not sure I—"

"The HOV lane," he asserts, straightening up with a pointed finger, "is prejudiced against those who don't have a family or the money to buy an electric car. The lonely and poor end up in bumper-to-bumper traffic on the 405 while the elite surpass us like they do in every other area of life." He waves his hands as he preaches, "MLK once said, 'One has a moral responsibility to disobey unjust laws.' The carpool lane is an unjust law. I wasn't trying to get home faster, Cal. It was a peaceful protest."

"What does the carpool lane's violation of your civil rights have to do with anything?"

"Cop pulled me over, and I used the civil rights explanation for my lawbreaking. He said he still had to write me a ticket, so I threatened to sue him for homophobia. He said he wouldn't recommend that since I would likely lose that suit against a gay officer, so I turned on the charm. Got a date and out of a $500 ticket. Now, will you try to keep up?"

What the hell am I supposed to be keeping up with?

He flicks his fingers my way. "Go ahead, Cal. Try to convince me you aren't happy your dad's career ended in a humiliating toilet flush."

Okay, so now we're back to talking about Estlyn and me?

"Just because Estlyn needed you doesn't

mean she doesn't want you." He takes a sip, then plunks his glass onto the bar. "Look, she hasn't dated anyone since college, and that guy bled to death in her arms. She won't admit it, but she's nerv—"

Holy shit. I shake my head. "I'm sorry. *What? How?*"

"Google Michael Bishop. That'll tell you everything."

Oh, shit. Shit, shit, shit! The guy the police shot in front of her was her boyfriend?

"All I'm saying is," Dean continues, either unaware of or unperturbed by my blood-drained face, "if you like her at all, give her another chance. She's not a normal human woman, so…" After taking a drink, he tilts his head side to side to contemplate his next words. "Adjust your expectations."

He lifts his butt from his chair enough to pull out a wallet, then hands me his credit card. "I gotta run. Estlyn's going on a date with this sleazebag attorney tonight. I have to squat at her apartment to make sure he doesn't try any funny business. Also, I'm out of beer at my place."

A date with someone else? Already? What the fuck? Why was she at Whitney's this morning? My throat stings at the thought of some other guy all over Estlyn. Or insider her.

"When are you heading over there?"

A smirk creases Dean's left cheek. Did I really just take the jealousy bait? Whatever. I get to see Estlyn. And that asshole she's going out with does not get to see her naked because I'm technically still her boyfriend for the next sixteen days.

"Come over any time after eight."

SIX

Estlyn

Fifteen Days Prior

I'VE NEVER FELT SO safe in a car. Sure, the Ken doll driving it makes me want to gouge my eyes out like Oedipus, but let's face it, he's a white DDA in Los Angeles. We're fucking invincible.

In front of the bar, I open the passenger door even as he races around the car to get it. Let the message be sent: *This date will end at my front door.* But he *will* have to pay for my drink because I'm at the tail end of a riches-to-rags story.

Remember when Young told me the police would return all my belongings? Remember how I also said he was full of bullshit? Well, here's the first place his cow shat. Yes, Rory and I were released. Yes, I have my apartment and all my devices back. Yes, I can use my credit cards. No, I no longer have a bank account with more than the minimum amount to keep it open. No, I no longer have eighteen grand in cash hidden away in my safe. I get the rest of my payment from the Mia Sanchez case this week, and hopefully, I get a deposit from the Rush case tomorrow. Until then, I'm broke.

Quin scoots his chair toward our cocktail table and says, "So, I heard you've been a little naughty lately."

Naughty? Are we in an erotic Christmas song? "Yeah?" I comb my fingers through the hair above my ear then flip it behind my shoulder. "What did you hear?"

"That the SWAT team found enough smack in your apartment for all of them to get high."

My eyebrows rise. "Oh, really?'

His lips slip into a smug grin. He thinks he's playing my Fifth Amendment right game. I'm not playing. No one mentioned drugs during my arrest. "They found six bindles in your safe."

Oh, please. That's not enough for them *all* to get high. Not that I would know. I'm not a drug user. "I'm sorry, do I look like someone who uses heroin?" I present the undersides of my elbows and even roll my tongue against the back of my top teeth to show my healthy veins. "I'm happy to show you between my toes if necessary."

"There's another common place you could inject—"

"Excuse me?"

He shakes off my spite and shrugs. "Dillon, you know they don't need any evidence that you used it. Possession is a misdemeanor—"

"Good evening," the waiter cuts in as he sidles up to our table.

Before he can say anything else, I order. "Two gin martinis, wet, shaken." I say thanks and pat his shoulder to excuse him from our presence, then turn back to my date.

"Quin, I didn't possess it. My brother's mom died from that shit. Why would I go anywhere near it?"

Quinton scoffs as he repeats the line every cop has heard a million times, "It wasn't my heroin. It was just locked in my safe." Okay, maybe not the locked safe part. I'm not sure where other people stash their heroin. "Dillon, come on."

"Are you fucking kidding me? This is the first I'm hearing about this!"

He puts his hands up in defense. "Look, I have scotch in the afternoon to get through—"

"Quinton," I growl, "they didn't charge me with possession. They seized my assets."

In other words, I have no right to anything they took. I have to go to court and prove nothing they seized is related to the drugs in any way, which is going to be pretty damn hard to do against any DDA working under Young. By the way, that's every DDA.

I drop my face into my hands and rub circles in my temples. "That son of a bitch had them plant it," I mutter. Young had to make sure hard drugs were in my apartment if he wanted the police to legally steal everything I owned. We're teetering on the edge of five years since Rory and I did that frame-up, so the cops couldn't take anything in the name of embezzlement charges. But throw some drugs in the mix and have them find more than $25,000 in assets, and my shit is all theirs—theirs until Young wants me to have it back.

"You're going with the 'police framed me' defense? Dillon, you're smarter than that."

I jab my finger in his direction, "And you're smart enough to know the police have been caught planting evidence when they're raiding a rich-enough person's property," I snap, pointing at myself.

"I've never understood how you bleeding hearts could be so paranoid. Aren't you supposed to believe there's good in everyone or some bullshit like that?"

"Quinton, does it happen or doesn't it?"

His eyes shut before he acquiesces. "It has once or twice in the past, but you really think the DA would—"

"*Thank you*. You owe me an apology for saying I'm paranoid."

"I'm sorry," he says with a sigh. "Look, I believe you."

"Really? Without checking between my toes?"

He reaches for my hand on the table. I let him hold it, rub his perfectly manicured thumb along it. Men's hands should not be this soft. "Can I help you get your stuff back?"

Gee, I thought you'd never ask.

With dreamy, *you're my knight in shining armor* eyes, I say, "You'd do that?" The waiter stops to set a martini in front of each of us. "Oh," I slide his martini to my side of the table, "they're both for me. Scotch neat, right?"

His flawless teeth appear in a wide grin before he turns to the waiter. "Whatever the lady asks for." When the waiter leaves, his pale fingers resume caressing mine. "Go easy on the police, okay?"

It's like he's forgotten who he's talking to.

My lips part to retort when he adds, "The opioid issue around here is a nightmare."

With the hand Quin isn't restraining, I pick up my glass and sip. "Oh?"

"The shit is everywhere. I can't tell you how many moms we've had to bring in to identify their kids' bodies after they've overdosed." He shakes his head. "God, I'm sick of it."

Huh. The guy might actually have a heart. It's small and dry-ice cold, but it could be somewhere buried in the hollow of his ribcage. Before I can stop it, my hand squeezes his. "That's awful. How long has it been this bad?"

"Uh, it wasn't great when I started working for my predecessor. But by the time I became DDA this year, we were up against an epidemic."

The waiter sets Quin's drink on the table, giving me an excuse to escape his grasp. Quin's disenchanted eyes settle on his empty hand before it lifts his drink to his lips.

"Why is it so bad?"

"Oh, it's okay," he waves me off. "You don't want to talk about work."

"No, no, this is interesting." Interesting if it gets my stuff back.

He folds his hands on the table and leans in. "Well, you probably know that most of the West Coast's heroin is from Mexico."

"No, I'm not particularly up on where my heroin comes from." I wink.

A smile cracks his cheek. "There's a newer cartel we've been watching, La Familia Gaviria. These guys have muscled out all the other suppliers in San Diego, Orange, and Los Angeles Counties. They're working on Riverside, too."

"Damn."

"Anyway, for whatever reason, their suppliers are almost impossible to catch. The few times we've gotten one in custody, Young offers a walk-free plea deal to give up the others. And every time the intel they've given us has been wrong."

"Wait, why is he letting them go before he verifies their intel?"

He swallows a sip of scotch, then lets the glass dangle from his fingers. "Well..." His eyes sweep the dim ceiling above. "The intel isn't *wrong*. It's just late. Like we spooked them, or like they got tipped off somehow." He lifts a finger from his glass and extends it my direction. "For instance, this one time a supplier we had in custody told us about this massive shipment they had coming in at the Port of LA."

"Yeah?"

"Well, it was where he said it would be, but no one picked it up. But because he held up his end of the bargain, we had to let him go."

"Ah." I nod.

"I don't know why Young keeps insisting we do those deals," he mutters.

I might have an idea.

QUINTON INVITED ME TO his place for a nightcap. After we left a *bar*. Subtle.

I declined.

When I get home, there's a handwritten note taped to the outside of my apartment door: *Don't have a heart attack. People are on your couch.*

I push the door open to Dean sipping a Corona with his feet up on my coffee table. He's watching a baseball game. Dean would never willingly put on a baseball game. "Is Rory here?"

He glances over his shoulder. "No, why?"

I must have just missed him then. Fine by me. I'm not in the mood to deal with Rory running interference between Olivia and me. *I'm sorry, Dil,*

I know you don't want to hear this again, but Liv asked me to talk to you. Have you thought about Christmas? How are we going to explain to our kid when you aren't there?

Well, Ror, tell the kid I'm with my dad. Tell him life is disappointing and it'll be better if he understands that sooner rather than later. Oh, and while you're at it, Rory, tell the little shit who else couldn't make it because he's dead.

No, I don't really want to say that. I'm sure my niece or nephew will be cute, and I'll love 'em and all, but that kid is already trying to upend the balance in my family. It's like Liv is trying to babyproof me. I'm sorry, but my brother's ejaculate creation won't obligate me to put bumpers on my sharp edges.

"That better not be one of my beers," I tell Dean as I kick off my heels. "You know I'm on a budget."

He flicks his fingers at me. "I'll give you a twenty before I leave."

"Why are you watching base—"

Oh. That's why. The bathroom door swings open, and Linus appears from behind it. Why is he in my apartment? Hanging out with Dean? When I wasn't here?

I need Dean's key back.

Linus freezes when he sees me, like he only planned up to this point and is hoping he can pause time until he figures out what to do next.

The tension feels thick, but it must not be that bad because Dean is still undisturbed on the couch—like it's *his* couch and he will not be interrupted by *not his* tension.

I snap the silence with, "You like the Dodgers?"

Linus cocks his head to the side as if my question is stranger than him being in my home uninvited. "No. I'm not really into sports."

Dean comes alive, throwing his hands in the air and letting them drop to his thighs with a slap. "Then why the hell are we watching this?"

"I don't know. You turned it on."

"You're a straight guy. I was trying to be polite."

Linus crosses his arms over his chest. "It's rude to stereotype, Dean."

"I'm sorry," I interject, dropping my purse on the coffee table, "why are either of you in my home?"

"I have a key," Dean answers.

Yes, Dean, I'm aware of the problem.

He tips his beer to Linus, whose hands are now hiding in his pockets. "Cal is here to cockblock that prosecuting prick."

Linus shakes his head. "That's definitely *not* why I said I was coming over."

"Oh, it was implicit." Dean lifts the remote to search Netflix, eager to disengage from the mess he orchestrated.

Linus's attention returns to me. "I'm here to make sure you don't have another heart attack." He points to my room, then puts his balls on the line with, "You're supposed to be resting. Go change and get in bed."

"Wow." I swipe Dean's beer and sit on the arm of the couch. "That was precious." I guzzle a mouthful before Linus yanks the bottle from my mouth.

"Now, Estlyn."

"Linus, you've done your due diligence. I didn't have sex with that prosecutor"—because there are few acts that would repulse me more. "You can leave now."

"Dean?"

"Yep." Without another word or even a glance in our direction, Dean stands, grabs his wallet and keys, and walks out the door.

Traitor.

Now it's just the two of us in a cage match, but it's my cage and Linus won't get out of it. So I guess it's more like a hostage situation in my own home.

"I promised your dad I'd take care of you," he asserts, "so you can choose to cooperate or not, but you're going to rest. And—"

"Oh, suddenly you're in the mood to make good on your promise?"

"And why didn't you tell me that your dad is in prison?"

I groan into my hands. "I'm gonna kill Dean."

"Dean didn't tell me that. I got a call today from an inmate at a California State Prison."

"Why did you answer?"

He shrugs. "If it was a wrong number, I thought I should let the guy know. Aren't those calls expensive?"

Damn it, that's kind of cute.

"Anyway, he called because he said you've been acting weird when you two talk and wanted to make sure you were okay."

"What'd you say?"

He sighs. "I said I was sorry, that I wasn't staying with you anymore."

"What'd he say?"

"He hung up."

I don't do anything to restrain the smile dancing across my lips. *That's right, Dad. Don't waste your precious phone minutes on Linus.*

Taking a deep breath, I say, "Look, my father is the most incredible man I've ever met. He's patient and brilliant and kind. But no one can hear any of that after the words *prisoner* or *felon* or, you know, *murderer*."

Linus's lips part for a moment, then shut—shocked but pretending that all his past girlfriends' dads were convicted of homicide, that he can handle this, that he's not judging. *It's okay. You can judge. Everyone else does.*

"So, no. I didn't tell the guy I had known

less than two weeks that my dad is locked up for twenty-five years with other"—insert air quotes—"*violent criminals* like himself. Why are you even bringing this up? If you're looking for another lie to accuse me of, this isn't one."

Linus steps toward me, closing the gap between us. My eyelids fall when his hands run down my arms, when his fingers twist with mine. I let them. I let them because I miss his hands. His hands are new and familiar. They're warm and rough. They entice a hunger in my skin and an urgency in my pulse.

The last hands that could do that grew cold in mine.

"That's why your dad's always so worried about you?" Linus asks. "Because he can't get to you if something happens?"

I study Linus's ivory fingers surrounding my pigmented ones. I feel his gaze as I turn our hands over and back again, taking in what it looks like to be held by him. My finger roams over the small mole on his right ring finger. It's darker than the freckles on the back of his hand. He has even more freckles on his arms and shoulders. Michael didn't have any freckles. He didn't have a mole on his ring finger. His palms weren't the same color as the rest of his hands. They were lighter, closer to the color of my skin. I flip our hands over. Linus's hands are the same color front and back.

"Yeah, I guess."

"And because you could have been killed that night, too, when Michael—"

"Nope. Don't." I pull my hands from not-Michael's and shake my head. "You don't get to talk about Michael, okay?"

"Okay, okay," he whispers as he retreats. His hands slide in his pockets before he rocks back on his heels. "So, uh, I'm going to stay." He pauses to comb his fingers through his dishwater hair. "I'll be on the couch if you… if you need anything."

I nod before heading to my bedroom and shut the door once I'm inside.

SEVEN

Cal

FOURTEEN DAYS PRIOR

ESTLYN'S SAFE BEEPS WHEN it unlocks. It's a soft, high tone that signals the correct six-digit code has been entered. It clicks when it opens. The first noise wakes me. The second jolts me.

I flick on the lamp above my head and allow myself to exhale. It's just her.

Estlyn doesn't acknowledge me or the light now illuminating the living room. In an oversized T-shirt and panties, she sits and stares into the empty safe. After a minute, her hand wanders inside it, feeling the bare walls and floor as if she'll find something.

She sighs and says, "It wasn't a date."

"Oh."

That's it. That's all I say. Because waking up to check an empty safe goes in the *strange-ass behavior* column. I wait for her to turn to me, to show me more than just her profile, but she just stares at the safe as if an object will suddenly appear inside.

"He's a DDA—the guy I met tonight," Estlyn says. "I asked him if he could get back what the police took from me."

I thought they just searched her stuff. I didn't know they took anything. Her staring into a safe with nothing inside makes a little more sense if it had been recently emptied without her permission. A *little* more sense. Not enough for this to be normal behavior.

What'd been in it? Evidence that linked her to a crime? Money? Fake IDs? Estlyn seems like the kind of person who would have a half-dozen alias passports stashed away somewhere.

"Is he going to?" I ask.

Her willowy arms wrap around her legs, pulling her knees to her chest. She buries her face in the crook of her elbow and sighs. A few silent seconds pass before I see a tear slip over her forearm and drip to the floor.

Well, this is clearly a no-win situation. I don't know that I have the right to touch or hug or comfort her. But if I do nothing, I'm the jerk who sat and watched her cry. Okay, Dean said Estlyn is not a normal human woman. What would give her some solace?

I start for her bedroom and rip the sheet and pillows off the bed. On my way back, I drag a dining chair to the living room and drape the sheet over it, tucking one edge behind the back of the couch and piling books on top of the coffee table to secure the opposite hem. When I go to grab the pillows from the floor, I notice Lioness has fallen out of the sheets onto the living room rug. I pick him—boy lions have manes despite what Estlyn says—up and offer the soft animal to her.

Estlyn's face lifts to mine before she takes it from my hand, her fingers brushing mine.

A few of the novels we picked up from the library are on the shelf below the TV. I sort through a pile and ask, "What tent do you want to go to? It looks like we have something murdery..." I move to the next one. "Wow, another murdery one, something courtroom with murder—obviously—and, huh..." I flip the paperback over to read the synopsis. "Oh..." I shamefully singsong. "You read smut."

She scoffs. "No, I don't."

I flip through it. Sure enough, amongst cheesy dialogue and over-narrated emotion, there is a lot of *sweat* and *moaning*, adjectives like *dizzy* and *wet*, and fingers and dicks *thrusting* in various orifices. "Estlyn, this is smut."

She spins on her butt to face me. "I agree. You said I *read* smut. But you have no evidence—"

"You checked it out at the library!"

"Circumstantial. *And*," she adds, the pitch of her voice rising defensively, "that's a really well-respected author!"

A soft chuckle hits the roof of my mouth.

"Well, I'll be in this tent," I point to the smut cover, "if you want to join me." I toss the book and a few pillows under the sheet, then crawl in after them. My head on a pillow, I flip open the cover and start reading about a couple who will go through the preformulated romance plot which guarantees they end up together. It's bad writing, but I'm just not in the mood for murder tonight.

Five pages in, Estlyn sweeps through my periphery to lie on the pillow beside me. She holds one of the murdery books above her face. We remain this way for several more pages until she whispers, "Linus?"

My face turns to hers, but she keeps reading. "Yeah?"

"Are you going to be here in the morning?"

My chest aches at the smallness of her voice. God, I fucked up last week. I actually hurt her. I didn't know I was capable of that. I didn't know anyone was. "Do you want me to be here?"

She shrugs.

"Then I'll be here."

I don't read more than a sentence before Estlyn snatches the smut I was ironically, of course, getting sucked into. She tosses the book aside and slides her foot over my legs. Once she's on top of me, her face lowers to mine. My eyes close when I expect to feel her lips, but they never touch mine. "Leave whenever you want. Just tell me first, asshole."

I open my eyes to her teasing ones. "You can ruin my father's life, just let me help next time."

"Okay," she breathes before our mouths collide.

EIGHT

Estlyn

FOURTEEN DAYS PRIOR

IT'S INCALCULABLY WRONG TO compare Linus and Michael, but I do. I am comparing.

The night I brought Linus home, he didn't waste any time with me. He knew exactly what he wanted, and he did it. My absurd display of dominance at the bar dissolved the moment he pressed me against the kitchen counter. And he shed his sensitive, just-dumped writer vibe when I stripped his shirt from his arms and his pants down his hips. It was the first time I'd had sex with someone who didn't treat me like I was breakable—or worse, already broken—and holy shit, it was hot as fuck.

I know. I'm a terrible person for even thinking that.

I love Michael. I loved the feel of his lips on my skin and how air escaped my lungs when he entered me. I loved how safe I felt surrounded by the strength of his body. And I loved his caution with my story, the care with which he handled me.

But I love that Linus touches me as if I could break him just as easily as he could break me. Because that's what sex is—removing every barrier, every piece of clothing between us until we're both naked and vulnerable, until we each can say *I'm giving you the power to hurt me. That's how much I want you.*

I realize now that Michael never offered me that part of him. He was so busy trying to make me feel secure and loved that he never showed me how to do the same for him. He could have. He would have, I know, if we'd had more time.

I squeeze Linus's fingers tangled in mine and stare past our extended hands to the open safe. We're lying on the couch under the sheet from the fort we destroyed. My back is against his bare chest, the sweat between our skin cooling as we share drowsy breaths.

My eyes can't leave the safe.

"He was going to propose," I whisper.

Linus's voice is groggy when he says, "What?"

Shit. I woke him up. I forgot he's an immediate postcoital sleeper. "Nothing."

"No..." He draws a reluctantly alert breath. "What did you say?"

"Michael. I found a ring when I was packing up our apartment after he died."

Linus's free hand covers my stomach, urging

me back against him. That's his entire response. He doesn't say anything. Fair. I told him he wasn't allowed to talk about Michael.

"I asked his family about it. They knew, but they didn't want to tell me. Thought it would hurt worse. My dad told me Michael even drove out to Lancaster to get his blessing." My lungs shudder as I inhale. "The police took the ring from my safe when they arrested me."

My body sinks backward when Linus pushes up on his hand and hovers over me. "Are you fucking kidding me? How can they do that?"

"I'm just telling you because I don't want you to think I'm this upset over some lost cash."

"I wouldn't blame you if you were." He shakes his head. "But you can get it back, right?"

I shrug and swipe a tear from my temple. He lies back down beside me and pulls me to his chest.

It should be Michael's chest.

The tears won't relent. My fists clench and my body tenses as I cry against Linus, each sob surging his scent into my lungs—his scent, not the one I'm desperate for.

That scent doesn't exist anymore.

But Linus holds me anyway. He strokes my hair and quiets me as I weep over losing a man we both know he'll never be.

Young's burner phone pings in my purse. The sun's already up when the sound opens my eyes to the sight of my living room covered in pillows, books scattered on the rug, and furniture in disarray.

The burner pings again.

Linus's arm is heavy over my waist when I reach for my purse on the coffee table. It's a message from a 323 area code.

Who did you choose?

I glance over my shoulder at the morning light warming Linus's sleeping face. His eyelashes rest above cheeks tanned from the summer sun. His hair is pointing wherever it wants, matching his boyish freckles more than the stubble on his jaw. I'm going to wake up to him tomorrow and the next day.

I will not wake up in prison.

I text back, *Working* on it.

The phone buzzes again. *I need a name by tomorrow.*

My God, I don't tell them how to run a gubernatorial campaign. Why are they breathing down my neck while I stage their homicide? Young's playing his hand, and I'm playing mine. He doesn't need to remind me when to bet or suggest how much to throw in the pot.

Yep, I reply.

"Babe," Linus murmurs, "I'm cold." His hand cups my hip before rolling me back to the warmth of his skin. After dropping the phone on the table, I relax as he wraps his arms around me.

"*Babe?* Does this trial run include pet names now?"

"Apparently," he stretches his morning voice as his nose brushes my neck. "I thought Dean gave you all your stuff back. Why do you still have a burner?"

Uh…

I told Dean the police didn't have enough evidence to charge us. I told Rory he had nothing to worry about, that if anything came up, I'd make it go away. I haven't told anyone the truth. Legally, I can't, even as I commit murder.

I turn to face Linus. My gaze climbs to his eyes, Heineken-bottle green stitching to aqua around his irises. "I lied to you."

His expression is hesitant, halfway between grateful for my honesty and understanding the irony of that gratitude. "About what?"

"About why the police released me."

"Okay."

"And I'm going to keep lying to you."

"For how long?"

"Good question." I click my tongue against the roof of my mouth as I think. "Indefinitely."

"Okay."

"Still want to call me *babe*?"

The skin between his eyes wrinkles a moment. "Yeah, I do."

Our gazes lock, and I nod slowly in case he

changes his mind. "Okay. I gotta get to work. Need a blanket?"

"No, I gotta get up. Meeting with Whitney and the producer."

"Producer?"

A sheepish smile curls half his lips. "I sold my screenplay."

I shove his chest. "Holy shit! With or without asides?"

"Without," he laughs.

"Why didn't you tell me?"

"I just did."

"Isla Jackson," I introduce myself as I extend my hand to Mrs. Rush. I'll admit that Emory isn't who I expected her to be. She's not a frumpy doormat of a stay-at-home mom, neither is she a suntanned carrot with brittle blonde hair sitting limply on her silicone knockers. She's a natural beauty—conservative makeup, dark hair up in a messy bun, flyaways held back by a knotted bandana. Her shocking blue eyes peek above the freckles splattered across her sun-kissed skin. The only thing fake about her is the ink on her slender arms. Her tattoo sleeves reach up to her shoulders, and more images peep out from beneath the racer back of her tank top.

She's the white version of cool.

Emory forces a smile when she says, "Thanks

for meeting with me."

"Can I get you something to drink?"

She smirks. "If it's included in the fee, hell yeah."

After I return to the table with our coffees, I start the usual process: nondisclosure agreement, feminine touch to remind the client I'm not a mob boss, and the semi-rhetorical question, "How are you holding up?"

"I'll be better when this is over."

I nod. "Ms. Rush…" It's important not to address the client as missus at these kinds of meetings. "I have a two-part service. First, I ensure that your husband experiences appropriate consequences for his indiscretion. Second, I provide you with some sort of restitution to alleviate the pain he caused you."

"Okay."

"So," I clasp my hands on the table, "let's tackle that first one. What would you like to happen to your husband?"

She purses her lips and searches the room behind me for an answer. "I want the thing most precious to him to collapse. And I want him to watch as it does and know there's nothing he can do to stop it."

My kind of girl. I jot a note on my legal pad. "And what is that?"

"His career."

"As a vascular surgeon?"

She nods. "We got married right before medical school. I supported him through nine years of training with shit-to-no pay. I raised his two kids and brought in an income of my own to keep the lights on while he went to school. Not to mention, I booked all his flights for his residency interviews. I scrimped and saved for his travel expenses and licensing exams. I proofread his research papers and application essays. I fucking ironed his shirts and made his lunches every day." If it wasn't obvious, her volume has doubled in decibels since she started.

"Do you happen to have his work contract?"

"Yeah." Emory passes me a thick envelope. "You should find everything you need in there."

I pull the papers to check her thoroughness. Marriage certificate, prenuptial agreement, Miles Rush's physician contract with UCLA Medical Center, the couple's joint investment portfolio, bank statements with highlighted expenses related to his affair, phone records with his mistress's number highlighted, screenshots of his mistress's Facebook and Instagram profiles, and—

"I won't be needing this," I say as I hand her back Miles's life insurance information.

"Oh," Emory perks up with a blush in her cheeks. "I thought you'd need to know how much we were worth, so he wouldn't get all our money when I leave him. You know, because of the prenup."

Right. There are still a few decent people in the world. Not everyone wants me to bring them a dead body between my teeth like a fucking Labrador.

I chuckle softly and tuck the insurance document back in the pile. "So, you want his career ruined. Anything else? Does…" I glance at the printed Facebook profile, "Reagan know your husband is married? Does he wear a ring?"

She shakes her head. "He doesn't wear a ring in the OR. Only when he's off work."

"If I find out she knew about you, is there anything you want me to do?"

Emory sits back, and her hands rotate the coffee cup that's now captivating her attention. "No," she finally sighs. "The girl's an intern. Surgery is so competitive. I doubt she felt she had a real choice."

Shit. This is the most empathic, least castration-minded infidelity client I've ever had. I kind of like her.

"And what do *you* want?"

"Our kids, our house, and enough alimony to supplement my income."

"What do you do for a living?"

"I'm a photographer. I do a lot of actor headshots. Sometimes album photography for musicians."

"Okay. Do you have a divorce lawyer?"

"Not yet." As I scribble a note, she adds, "I

want him to take his dumbass dog. Is that possible?"

I smile. "I'm sure you can take that up with your lawyer." I glance down at my notepad. "And does your husband have any professional or personal enemies?"

She snickers. "He's a vascular surgeon. They're all enemies."

"Perfect."

NINE

Cal

Fourteen Days Prior

Two can lie.

There is no meeting. I'm back at Elliot's making calls to every LAPD station in the area, trying to track down Estlyn's ring. I know if I call and say *Hey, assholes, you took my temporary girlfriend's engagement ring that her boyfriend was going to give her before one of yours shot him to death,* they'll probably hang up. So, I'm just trying to find the one they took her to when they arrested her. I've called every station. None of them will tell me anything.

I open the bar again today, which is equivalent to drawing the short straw. Openers get the shittiest tips, but at least I have nights free to spend my no money.

It's four when Dean knocks on the bar like it's a door.

"Is day drinking part of your job or something?" I ask as I set a tumbler on the bar.

"I got a tip that Portia de Rossi day drinks here."

"Really?"

"No. But you guys have great air conditioning." I slide him his whiskey neat before he adds, "Hey, when are you going to offer me a drink on the house? Or do I have to sleep with you to get that?"

"Estlyn doesn't even get free drinks. Oh, and speaking of Estlyn," I say, leaning toward him, "you're a well-connected person with questionable morals—"

"I prefer *popular* and *ethically liberated*, but…" He waves his hand to urge me to continue before he takes a sip.

"Do you know how to get something the police confiscated?"

He purses his lips, crinkling his brow. "It depends. Which 'police' and what 'something?'"

"The LAPD and the engagement ring Michael bought for Estlyn."

Dean's eyes widen, then roll as if to shake off the significance of what I just said. His hands run over the buzzed sides of his scalp, kneading out his frustration without disturbing the longer, styled hair on top. Even his agitation has to look good. "Shit," he murmurs beneath his breath. He thumps both elbows on the bar and brings his folded hands to his chin. If this seems like a lot of inexplicable fidgeting without enough verbal explanation, it's because it is. "Okay," he finally says to me, "there's the fast, cheap way we can handle this, or the long, probably expensive way that Estlyn would have to do it herself."

"Well, let's do the fast, cheap way." *Obviously*.
He cringes.
"Um, the long, expensive way, I guess?"
"I know an LAPD detective."
"That's amazing. Do you think he'd help us?"

He sighs the most melodramatic sound I've heard from an adult male. "Probably."

"Okay, then let's talk to him."

Dean takes another drink of whiskey but doesn't respond.

"Dean. Who is he?"

"You know that stereotype that cops are disgusting, cheating, lying sons of bitches?"

"Is that a thing?"

"Wyatt is that thing."

I press my crossed forearms into the bar and lean in for details. "So, he's your ex?"

"Do you know what ex means in Latin?"

"Out of." Yes, I *am* an impressive, prep-school kid.

"As in out of my life, out of my mind, and completely out of the question."

I'm not sure I've heard someone be so off the cuff poetic—or rehearsed—in their day-to-day speech. Dean makes me feel like I've been doing my everyday theatrics all wrong.

"Dean, it's *Michael's* ring."

He holds up a resolute finger, then wags it back and forth. "Uh-uh. I do not succumb to guilt trips, so don't waste your breath."

"Dean…"

"Look, if I do this, you get laid, and I binge a carton of Tillamook Mudslide while watching *My Best Friend's Wedding* on repeat."

"Isn't that movie, like, twenty years old?"

He glares at me, his spiteful eyes refusing to leave mine as he throws back the rest of his whiskey.

"Okay, there has to be a way we can do this without you binge-watching Julia Roberts—"

"Rupert Everett."

Fine. I'll concede. That British bloke is a stone-cold fox.

I comb my fingers back through my hair, then push up from the bar. That's when I have it. "Drinks on the house the rest of the year."

His right eyebrow arches. "An entire calendar year."

"Fine."

Another sigh of reluctance from Dean. "When does your shift end?"

I smile. "Six."

Dean slams his empty glass on the counter. "Another."

I take a breath and stare at the tumbler. The whiskey bottle is in my hand, but I don't fill his glass. "Dean," I say, lowering my voice, "do you drink like this all the time?"

Twice, he nudges his glass toward me with his fingertip. "Only when I have to see my ex."

"Look, I don't mean to overstep, but my mom's an alcoholic, and I—"

"Oh," he grins, "I don't have a problem with alcohol. In fact, we're on excellent terms." He takes the bottle and pours his own drink, more than two fingers.

Does he not remember that we're going to a police station before that'll be off his breath?

"But I think it's sweet you're trying to get between us so you don't have to fund our romance." Winking, Dean raises the glass to me in a one-sided toast. "To love that doesn't leave you for Ben. And to you pretending to be my boyfriend in front of Wyatt to rub it in his smug face."

"Yeah, I'm not doing that."

Rolling his eyes, he tries his toast again. "To you paying for my drinks."

I shrug. "Sure."

TEN

Estlyn

FOURTEEN DAYS PRIOR

I NEED TWO DEAD bodies, preferably white, ideally upper class.

I need one of Emerson's selected felons to kill, preferably murder, ideally with graphic brutality, these two white bodies. Or I need to at least fabricate enough evidence that a jury would believe the picture I'm going to paint beyond a reasonable doubt. Not that this case would go to trial. Young would personally draft a plea bargain that would drown the felon in charges until a jail cell would have more oxygen than a courtroom. These five men, these five files in front of me, are surely too poor to pay for an attorney. They'll plead guilty before they dial their phone call from the police station.

Two lives will be lost, and one life will essentially end. In exchange, two records will be expunged, and one man will be exonerated. Three lives for three lives. That's the deal.

I have three options to weigh: I can hire a hitman and plant evidence, kill two people myself then plant evidence, or provoke one of these felons to massacre a couple of white people.

I don't trust a hitman to handle my frame up, and I don't think I have the balls to murder anyone. Plus, that'd just prove all those foster families right who didn't want me because they thought I was inherently violent. I'm not violent. My dad isn't, either. It's not in our DNA. So, since killing isn't something I can do, I gotta get one of these guys riled up somehow—scared, pissed, or high enough to create a *Willie Horton* massacre of whatever rich people I put in his path.

I spread the fat felon files on my dining table in front of me, the ocean roaring outside the sliding door just beyond. It's always nice to have a view of the Pacific when plotting how to destroy someone's life. Young insists on using paper files to avoid leaving a paper trail. The first thing I did was put a sticky note over the name of each felon. These aren't people with names their mothers gave them. They are files. One of them will be a murderer.

In lieu of their real names, I have labeled their files by disgusting animals. I figure that will make this process more palpable. Those files are now labeled Cockroach, Pube Louse, Tarantula, Millipede, and Hamster—which is basically just a large, hairy bug. Their bites can kill humans.

People should know.

All of these animals have two strikes, and, for a felony to count as a first strike, it must be a *serious* felony. Think rape, murder, armed robbery, assault, molestation—the kind of felonies people like to watch prosecuted in courtroom dramas but go unpunished in gory films. I figure this will be easy. What are the chances that none of the five have held a gun to someone's head while stripping them of their clothes and/or possessions?

Apparently, the chances are pretty damn good.

The first *serious felony* of each of these men is selling or administering drugs to minors. I should have guessed. Young said Sellards specialized in defending drug offenders. *But come on, felons, give me a little help framing you here.*

I force my finger under the sticky note covering Cockroach's basic personal information. His birthdate was thirty-two years ago. His first strike, thirteen years ago. At the age of nineteen he offered a girl some ecstasy at a party. The girl was sixteen. An undercover cop was in attendance. Cockroach's second offense was possession. I fold his file closed and drop it in the box on the dining chair next to me.

All right, Pube Louse, sell some smack to at least one twelve-year-old. The gubernatorial race is counting on you. I scan his file. So far, so good.

Looks like Pube Louse was a legitimate drug dealer. He was arrested and sentenced to five years in prison for selling pot to multiple high school students on school grounds. His second was possession of crack shortly after his release from prison, and he was arrested a third time a couple of weeks after being released again. He was acquitted of that third crime thanks to Young's opponent's free legal defense. My finger slides beneath the pink note covering his birthday. This guy is twenty-nine. His first offense was when he was only eighteen. He has spent only two years of his adult life out of a cell. I put him in the *maybe* pile.

Tarantula and Millipede both have a personal affinity for opioids, which they are quick to share with others—illegal-prescription and heroin, respectively. Hamster manufactured and distributed meth to teens and adults alike.

Hamster looks promising. Sure, his last strike-worthy conviction was fifteen years ago, but how can I feel bad for framing a guy for murder who robbed so many people of their brains and teeth? A quick Google search reveals that, not only is he a reformed convict, he helped start a drug treatment program for low-income patients.

Well, fuck you, Hamster.

I slide Hamster's file into the box with Cockroach. Heroin doesn't make a user agitated or paranoid. Crack does. I think Pube Louse is going to have to be my coked-out villain. Now I just have to figure out how to turn a high into a murderous rage.

I stash the other two files away in the box, then study Mr. Pube Louse, whose real name I now have to subject myself to.

Xavier Freeman.

Twenty-nine years old, son of Victoria Freeman, former student at Centennial High. Currently working at In-n-Out in South Gate, where he has been steadily employed for the last eighteen months. It may seem like a shitty gig to work at a fast-food restaurant, but In-n-Out has damn good pay and benefits. And French fries. If he's held a job there this long, he's probably clean.

How the hell am I supposed to get a decent human who isn't high to kill two strangers? And how do I get two upper-class white people to an In-n-Out in South Gate? In-n-Out, sure, but to South Gate? Rich whites don't just drive their Bentleys through South Central. Not ones with intact mental health, at least.

My nails drum against the table top as I fight the urge to reconsider the other felons. It's like Young's so confident in his Texas Hold'em hand he's giving me the chance to pick between five different flops. But whatever three cards I choose for Young and I to share on the table, I still hold two number cards in my hand that are different suits, different values, and too far apart for a straight. So even though I get to pick the flop, I'm trapped at the table with that shitty hand and all my chips in the pot—which Young stole and tossed there. Folding isn't an option. Praying that the turn and the river save me is. Convincing him I have a pair of aces would do, too.

I grab the burner phone and type a message back to Young, or more likely, Emerson.

Xavier Freeman.

I chuck the phone into the file box and exhale a slow breath with my eyes shut.

ELEVEN

Cal

FOURTEEN DAYS PRIOR

"HOW LONG WERE YOU two together?" I whisper to Dean in the lobby of Detective Wyatt Kelly's station. With a name like that, I'm not sure Wyatt had any choice but to become a police officer. I hope he has a cop mustache. Mostly, I'm just boiling over with curiosity about who would survive a romantic relationship with Dean. I mean, he's great and all, but high-maintenance as hell.

"Too long," Dean huffs as he pushes through the door to the detective offices.

The receptionist glances up at us, breaking into a snicker-giggle when she sees Dean.

"I don't want to hear it, Tiffany," he growls. Dean tilts his chin up, strides down the linoleum aisle between desks, and drops into a chair next to one with the name plate *Det. Wyatt Kelly* displayed prominently on the front corner. Leaning his elbow on the desk, he rests his head in his hand, his fingers pressing into his temple and thumb into his jaw. His eyes close for a moment before glancing my way as he lets out another why-did-you-drag-me-here sigh.

I stand in front of the desk, unsure what to do with my hands. Or the rest of my body. Did I mention no one is behind the desk? We're just hanging around an empty desk that supposedly belongs to Dean's ex-boyfriend.

Finally, a clean-shaven—*damn it*—detective in a white dress shirt and blue tie emerges from another room and sits down at the desk. He's not as striking as Dean—well-groomed, but not with the same precision—but he's tall and broad shouldered, with blue eyes and light brown hair. And he doesn't seem to give a fuck that his ex-boyfriend is at his desk. His voice is flat and professional when he rests his folded hands on the desk and asks, "How can I help you, gentlemen?"

Dean's hazel eyes roll as he snaps his tongue. "Really?"

"I was about to head out, but—"

"On your way home to see Ben?" Dean retorts.

"Sir," I interject, then immediately wish I hadn't. Dean's fuming eyes dart to mine.

Okay, I guess the reason we came here can wait.

Wyatt's attention narrows on me. "Detective Kelly," he says, introducing himself as he stands and offers me his hand. "What can I do for you?"

I shake it and try to shrug off Dean's glare even though it's still punching me in the face. "Sir, my girlfriend's apartment was raided last week. The LAPD took everything from her safe, including the engagement ring her deceased boyfriend was going to give her. Is—"

"The boyfriend one of your buddies shot four times," Dean berates. "Michael Bishop. Do you remember him, or is it too hard to keep track of the black men you all have shot?"

Jesus, could Dean make this more uncomfortable? Apparently he could, because Wyatt seems unfazed. I've known the guy thirty seconds, but I can already tell he has the exact personality needed to date a guy like Dean.

"Is your girlfriend Dillon Collins?" he asks without so much as twitching in Dean's direction.

I nod.

Wyatt pivots to his computer and types. The silence is weird—Dean is fired up and trying to get everyone else to his level of agitation, Wyatt is calm and focused, and I have so many questions to ask Estlyn about Dean that I'm worried I'll lose track of them before I get home to her.

"Okay." Wyatt rubs his jaw and studies the screen. "Her charges were dropped, but the officers found heroin in her safe, so they confiscated everything in it as well as her bank accounts."

"Heroin?" I turn to Dean.

"Dillon doesn't do heroin," he scoffs. "She always says she wouldn't do drugs even if she were white enough to get away with it."

I pinch my lips together to hold in a laugh.

Wyatt folds his hands on the desk when he turns to us. "Well, they didn't charge her with possession or with intent to distribute, but legally, those assets are dirty. If she wants the ring back, she's going to have to sue for it."

My hand scrubs my forehead then draws down to my mouth as I think. No offense to Dean, but I could have come in here and heard this bad news from a detective without him. It's not like he's contributed anything but bitchiness to this meeting.

"It's not evidence, is it, Wyatt?" Dean asks in a shockingly pleasant tone.

"No, it's a civil forfeiture."

His fingertips press into the desk, shifting from left to right as he speaks. "So, you don't care about the ring, just the monetary value of it, right?"

Wyatt and Dean share a loaded gaze for several seconds. "Right," he finally agrees.

"How much can we pay you for it?" Okay, maybe I spoke too soon about Dean.

Sighing, Wyatt click-clacks on his keyboard. "They estimated the value to be eighteen thousand dollars."

Well done, Michael.

"Well, you won't get that if you pawn it. We'll

give you fifteen."

"Dean, you know I'd just give it back if I could, but it's not my case." Leaning in, he lowers his voice. "I shouldn't even be doing this."

"I can do eighteen," I chime in.

Their faces meet mine.

"I, uh…" My hand rubs the back of my neck as I try to figure out how to come up with eighteen thousand dollars. The producer is supposed to fork over the first fifty grand for my screenplay any day now. Until then, I only have eight thousand in savings. And an extra kidney. That's gotta be worth ten grand, right? "How long do I have to get you the money?"

"About three weeks," Wyatt answers. "Unless she decides to sue for her stuff."

"I'll have it to you by then."

TWELVE

Estlyn

Fourteen Days Prior

Xavier Freeman is on Facebook. He's also on Twitter and GoFundMe. The link to his GoFundMe page has been posted more than anything else on both of his social media feeds. All the captions on each link ask for prayers and contributions for somebody named Jayden's Cystic Fibrosis Treatment Fund. This Jayden kid appears to be on the cusp of adolescence in the photograph that repeats as I scroll down Xavier's Facebook profile. I click the link and read the fundraising description.

Thank you for your generous support of our son, Jayden, who was diagnosed with Cystic Fibrosis as an infant. CF is a congenital condition that causes his body's mucous to thicken. Because this happens in his lungs, Jayden struggles to breathe on a daily basis.

He is on the waitlist for a lung transplant. Even if he gets one, our savings won't be enough to pay the hospital bills. Our health insurance doesn't even cover the cost of all the treatments he needs right now.

All donations received will go toward Jayden's medical expenses. Any extra will go into a savings account for his transplant surgery. We appreciate every dollar you give. It means the world to us!

Beneath the description is a photograph of Jayden, a woman who I assume is his mom, and Xavier, who is slapping me in the face with a Hallmark-esque plea to have mercy on him and his sick kid.

Maybe I should look in the felon file box again. I could pick someone who doesn't have a diseased son with a short life expectancy. Because maybe Jayden is on Xavier's health insurance. If he goes to prison will Jayden have any coverage, or will he go on state insurance? What if he doesn't qualify for the free insurance, and his mom has to pay out-of-pocket premiums?

Nope. We've all got problems. I'm sure if I looked hard enough, I'd find a sob story in each of those felons' lives. It has to be Xavier. I already gave Young his name.

I no longer have the luxury of choice. Or of a conscience.

That tightening inside my chest returns, the kind that squeezed the oxygen from me the night of my heart attack. I hear each drumbeat of my pulse in my ears. Louder. Faster. Angrier. My eyes squeeze closed when my vision clouds with grey and black.

Fuck, is this another heart attack? I don't have time for that kind of shit right now!

The doctor gave me something for this, I think. Something to slow everything down.

I shove my chair out from the table and half-grope my way to the bathroom, clutching the doorframe to steady myself. I whip open the medicine cabinet and scan the contents until I find the little pills the doctor said would, and I'm quoting, *calm me the hell down*. Even after I pop one in my mouth, the room suffocates me. I make my way to the dining room, then slide open the door to my balcony. My hands grasp the railing, and my arms cross on it as I lean my chest over the edge.

Narrowing my view to the warm red of the inside of my eyelids, I listen to the ocean. I try to sync my breathing to the sound of the waves hitting the sand, but my lungs can't slow down. It's less suffocating out here, though. The air's better, what with the cool breeze sweeping off the Pacific. Each breath counts a little more than it did inside.

After several stifled inhalations, I finally catch my breath. I look up to see the sun shimmering off the water. The grey splotches fogging up my vision fade until I can see the ocean meet the blue sky in a crisp line.

A truck honks on the street below, yanking my attention a few hundred feet down. Nope. Shouldn't have looked down. Being reminded that I'm inches from a fatal fall isn't exactly soothing. I snap my eyes back to the horizon.

Hang on...

What was I thinking? Xavier isn't the wrong felon for this because his kid is sick. He's the perfect felon for this because his kid is sick. He has nothing to lose and everything to give.

I just have to convince him to give it.

THIRTEEN

Cal

Fourteen Days Prior

Estlyn gave me a key. It unlocked the door just fine, but I'm still not sure I'm in the right apartment when I step inside. There's no way to explain my hesitation at crossing the threshold without sounding like a racist jackass, but here it goes—country music is blasting from the bathroom. Country music. And not even that mainstream stuff that sometimes sneaks on a Top 40 radio station in Los Angeles. Drowning out the sound of her shower is twangy, Georgia-grown, beer-and-blue jeans music.

I freeze in the living room when the song ends—Miranda Lambert, I think. Or Carrie Underwood. Or any one of those other gorgeous blonde singers. Maybe it was a fluke. Maybe Estlyn's not listening to country music, just one country song ended up on her Pandora playlist. It happens to all of us. She thumbs-upped one genre-bending artist—Taylor Swift, maybe—and the rest of the white ladies from Nashville descended through her speakers. When the next song starts, I know that's not the case.

I drop my wallet and keys on the kitchen counter and knock on the bathroom door she left ajar. "Est," I shout over Dan + Shay, whose name I only know from seeing it on her phone. "Have you had dinner yet?"

She snatches back the curtain, revealing her dripping face and straightened hair preserved in a bun and thick headband. We stare at each other. I can tell she's fighting a smile as hard as I am.

"I, um…" she starts, then bites her full bottom lip. "I can explain this."

I take a step toward her. "Explain what?"

"It's just… I was an English major."

"Sure." I shrug. I'm dying to hear how this justifies the country music. Dying.

"So, I…" She takes a contemplative breath. "I appreciate good storytelling, which many music genres lack."

"Of course." I nod with exaggerated agreement.

"Country songs are poetry *and* concise stories. They elicit an emotional response from the listener in five minutes or less." Her pitch rises, words quickening like they did when she tried to defend her smutty book. "It's literary genius," she goes on, "and, frankly, doesn't get the credit it deserves."

I continue to nod as I listen to the lyrics playing from the Bluetooth speakers. "This song is about tequila."

"Poetry, damn it," she deadpans.

I chuckle as she grabs my shirt. Estlyn pulls me to her, her lips landing on mine. She tugs on the fabric covering my chest. "Why are you still dressed? Get in here."

I pull my shirt over my head. "Do we have to listen to this though?"

She laughs, a deceptively innocent sound, then shuts the curtain. "You can put on whatever you want as long as you take your clothes off."

Screw it. I'll endure country music for sex. I step out of my pants and into the shower. She doesn't flinch when I close the curtain behind me, keeping her eyes closed as she rinses off her body wash. Her hands follow the white bubbles that drift down her macchiato skin, over her slender shoulders, down the curve of her waist to her thighs.

I haven't looked at her naked body like this before, from a distance, like a Peeping Tom with permission. She's stunning—delicate and vulnerable and somehow still able to scare the shit out of me.

And I haven't really listened to the words to the song playing before this moment. It's not about tequila. Not really. It's about being haunted. It's about never getting over someone he can never get back. It's about a drink tearing loose a memory inside him that he always carries but one that only aches when he tastes tequila.

Damn it. That is good storytelling. Estlyn will never hear it from me.

I reach out to trace the curve of her hip. I grip her waist and pull her chest into mine. With my free hand, I tip her chin up. "Do you have a *tequila*?"

She squints and tilts her head at me. "Why? I thought you didn't drink."

"No," I snicker, "I meant the song. What reminds you of Michael?"

"You want to talk about the other guy who was inside me before you're about to be?"

Well, when you put it like that...

My thumb rubs over her cheekbone as I inch her back against the wall. "Just curious."

She steps her feet on either side of one of mine then slides her hand down my chest. Down my abdomen. Until I'm hard in her hands. "Peanut butter cookies."

I force my lungs to breathe through her touch. "Really?"

"And strawberry ice cream."

I shut my eyes and lean my forehead against hers. "Why?"

Her hands wrap behind my neck, then draw my mouth to hers. She sinks me into her kiss, her tongue and lips warm against the cooling drops of water on my skin. I grip her thighs to pick her up, pressing her back against the tile wall. My name releases from her lungs before I'm even inside her.

But she never answers my question.

FOURTEEN

Estlyn

Fourteen Days Prior

I'm trying to remember why I ever gave Dean a key.

I'm also trying to figure out if Jason Aldean is loud enough to cover the sound of Linus and I finishing. Because Jason couldn't muffle the sound of Dean slamming my apartment door and shouting something along the lines of, "I'm never helping you again, Cal!" It was hard to hear his exact words over all the soft screams echoing in the shower.

My breath isn't yet contained when I ask Linus, "Did you close the bathroom door?"

His forehead relaxes into the tile beside my ear. "No," he exhales.

I laugh in shallow bursts as I drop my feet to the tub. He kisses my cheek, then tucks my face against his chest. Linus is a cuddler, but Dean is sort of ruining the afterglow he's trying to bask in.

"My Lord," Dean yells again, "have some shame! Shut the door if you're going to fornicate."

Linus winces when I holler, "The door *was* shut. Text before you come over!" To Linus I add, "I'm sorry."

He shakes his head and turns off the faucet. "Don't be. I think this one's my fault."

I hand him a towel behind the curtain and wrap up in one myself. "What did you do?"

His voice hushes to a whisper when he asks, "What happened between Dean and his ex?"

"Wyatt?"

He nods.

"Linus. What did you do?" From the living room I hear that girly-ass—and, by the way, misogynistic—song that opens *My Best Friend's Wedding*. "Shit," I hiss before stepping out of the shower. My towel snug around my boobs, I stomp toward the couch and find exactly what I'd hoped I wouldn't—Dean in sweatpants and an LAPD T-shirt, huddled around a carton of Tillamook Mudslide ice cream. Why did that Oregon dairy brand ever infect Los Angeles? I half blame them for this.

I turn off the TV and spin to face Dean, my body blocking the screen.

"What the hell, bitch?"

"Give me the ice cream," I say, hands planted on my hips.

Dean glares at me as he shovels another bite into his mouth. He shows off the chocolate cream on his tongue as he barely articulates, "Ice cream is the consolation prize for people who don't get to have sex."

"Dean…"

He grabs the remote and flicks the television back on.

"What happened? Did he call you? Did you run into him?"

His eyes drift off my face to something behind me. I turn to see Linus with a towel around his hips. He makes a frantic dash into my bedroom, and definitely not because he's shy about seeing Dean after that little audio-sans-visual show we gave him.

"Linus! What'd you do?"

He shuts the door. He actually shuts me out of my own room.

"It's nothing," Dean says with a dismissive wave of his spoon. "Now, are you going to watch the best unrequited love movie of the nineties, or are you going to abandon me in the midst of my heartache?"

"No! I'm sorry, but you know I have no sympathy for you."

"Then why bother saying *sorry*?"

"I'm Team Wyatt on this one, and you know you're in the wrong if I choose a cop over you."

"Hold on—" The bedroom door behind me

busts open. "You said Wyatt cheated on you."

I throw my head back and cackle. "That's the story Dean told you?"

Dean snaps, "If it's not true, how come he's with Ben now?"

"Because he wanted to be with someone who wanted to be with him," I snap back. Turning to Linus, I explain, "Dean dumped Wyatt because Wyatt asked him to move in."

"After how long?"

"Two years."

Linus snorts and narrows his eyes on Dean. "And you made me feel so bad…"

"About what?" I interject.

Dean and Linus look at each other, and I can see they've decided to keep whatever secret they have from me. I am not a fan of this friendship, but I guess it was inevitable. Dean drinks religiously, and Linus offers communion and takes confession daily at Our Lady of Perpetual Inebriation.

"You never answered me earlier about dinner," Linus says, sidestepping my question. "Have you eaten yet?"

Fine, I'll bite. I don't have extra energy to expend on figuring out what they're talking about. "No."

"Do you want me to cook or pick something up?"

Cook? He's offering to *cook* for me? Better

not go that route. It's sweet, sure, but what if he can't? "Whatever's cheapest."

His hands find the small of my back and ease me closer to him. My eyelids lower when I feel his warm lips against my forehead. "I can get whatever you want, okay?" he whispers.

I scoff. "I can buy my own food."

He leans back and lifts my face to his. "Are you serious? Have you not noticed I'm a homeless guy living in your apartment rent-free? Let me buy you dinner."

"And some whipped cream," Dean adds.

I roll my eyes. "There's some in the fridge."

My phone rings, cutting off the music it was still playing in the bathroom. "Chipotle sounds good," I tell Linus before taking off to answer it.

My heart races when I see the contact lighting up my screen. *Please be good news. Please be good news.*

"Quin?"

"Dil, hey. Sorry it's late."

I pull my phone from my ear to look at the time. "It's nine o'clock. Is that late for someone in their thirties?" I tease, then close the bathroom door.

"Ha-ha. Look, I pulled those case files you wanted."

"Thanks, that's great. What'd you find?"

"So, there have been four arrests in connection with La Familia Gaviria. Like I said, they were all released without jail time, fines, or probation through plea bargains Young drafted."

"Okay. Were any of them deported?"

"All of them. They were also put on ICE and DEA watch lists."

"Okay." Something's missing here. I drum my fingers on the counter, searching my mind for the piece I need. "And none of their intel panned out?"

"Well, actually, some of it did. I told you about that Port of LA shipment, right?"

"The one that no one picked up because they got spooked?"

"Right. Okay, so there were two of those cases. And the other two, each perp tipped the cops to raid a home—one in Downey and one in Alhambra. Both houses were all but cleared out when the DEA got there. No cash, no drugs, no people, nothing. But it was obvious that whoever had been occupying the residences had recently hauled ass out of there."

"Those suppliers who snitched, were they out on bail?"

"No, their bail was revoked."

"What about phone calls? How were these guys tipped off if they were locked up?"

"All their calls were through the police line and recorded."

"Can I get those recordings?"

"Yeah, sure."

"Thanks." I nibble on my already short thumbnail. This is all what I need, but not all that I need. "Quin, who were their defense attorneys?"

"Uh, let me check." I hear some typing and clicking, then a pause. "Okay, this first guy's lawyer was someone named Emerson Brammer. And the others… Huh, they're all Emerson Brammer."

My teeth sink into my bottom lip. "Is there any way you can send those files to me?"

"Yeah, sure."

"Thanks, Quin."

"Hey, are you free this weekend for dinner? There's this new place up by the Getty—"

"I'm sorry, Quin. I'd love to, but my boyfriend and I just got back together."

"Oh." Awkward silence. "When?"

"This morning." For once I'm not lying, but my answer reeks of bullshit.

"Oh."

Please, please still send me those case files.

"I'll, uh, send those files and recordings your way. Let me know if you need anything else."

Thank God.

"I'm sure we'll be in touch. Thanks, Quin."

"Anytime." He hangs up before I can say goodbye.

FIFTEEN

Cal

FOURTEEN DAYS PRIOR

I COULDN'T HAVE BEEN gone more than half an hour, but that was plenty of time for Estlyn to fall asleep on the chaise portion of the couch. She's cuddled up with Dean who'd occupied the spot alone when I left. I'm still amazed at his ability to get her to fall asleep so fast.

God, she really is like a toddler.

That awful movie is only halfway over, but Dean is slowing down on the ice cream intake. I set our pseudo-Mexican food on the coffee table and sit next to him.

"She doesn't tolerate me bitching about Wyatt. *Ever*," Dean whispers, "but you opened the floodgates, so count on lots of venting at the bar over free whiskey."

I smile and roll my eyes while I sift through the bag for my chicken tacos. "Why doesn't she tolerate it?"

Estlyn stirs against Dean, then sighs a sleepy

breath when she settles with her cheek on his chest. He runs his hand down her arm—a sign of affection he would only show her in her unconsciousness—then returns his attention to me. "I can count the people she trusts on one hand. That's her circle, her pack. She's not above lying or blackmail or exploiting people, but never those people. She'll run with them off a cliff or into a prison cell. Those people—those people and her job—she'll bend the world for." He points his spoon at me. "You know. You saw her get arrested for what she did for Michael."

"What she did for Michael?"

He shakes his head and digs back into his ice cream. I'm not sure he realizes how often he does that—answers a question with a head shake. *That's not an acceptable answer, Dean.*

"As I was saying, Estlyn's loyal. So, she's not a fan of my aversion to commitment. She just doesn't get it. Whenever I told her it was just too fast with Wyatt even though I loved him, she would say she'd give anything to have Michael back and that I was, quote, 'a whiny, ungrateful pussy who didn't deserve love.'"

"Whoa."

"Well, she was grieving, and that shit isn't pleasant."

"When did you guys break up?"

"January."

She was grieving up until this year? Why the

sudden need to take a stranger home from a bar? And if she didn't need me for a case, why did she pick me?

After half a bite of ice cream, Dean adds, "He started dating Ben in March."

"Damn. That's quick."

He turns to me and smirks. "Didn't you sleep with Estlyn after you had been single only a month?"

"Yeah, but that's different. That was a one-time thing."

He scoffs and rolls his eyes. "Clearly."

"You know what I mean."

"And what is it now?"

"A four-week thing."

"So what happens in, what—two weeks?"

I let out a deep breath. "I don't know."

Dean studies me a moment and nods. He drops his spoon in the ice cream carton and hands it to me. I follow his silent order to set it on the coffee table. When I turn back, he ushers me over to where he's sitting and gingerly slides away from Estlyn's side. I take his seat and relax my arm behind Estlyn's back. She rolls onto my chest, shifting her shoulders and nuzzling her cheek against my T-shirt.

Dean kicks back beside me and whispers, "She wouldn't want to waste any time with me then."

SIXTEEN

Estlyn

THIRTEEN DAYS PRIOR

I DON'T REMEMBER GETTING into bed last night. I don't remember my head against Linus's shoulder as he carried me to my room. I don't remember my face meeting the pillow or him pulling the covers up to my shoulders. I don't remember him crawling under the sheet beside me. And I don't want to remember a time when he didn't.

My fingers are careful not to wake Linus as I stroke a few strands of his hair back into place. Michael was a light sleeper and an early riser. I almost never got to see him with his eyes closed next to me. Most mornings, I woke up to his kiss on my cheek and his voice reminding me I would be late for class or court if I didn't get up. A couple of times, I woke to a text saying he kissed me but I probably wouldn't remember.

God, I wish I had woken up then.

Linus doesn't stir when I leave the bed. I ease my bedroom door shut and start a pot of coffee without switching on the kitchen lights. This is my favorite time of day. The dawn sun is enough to illuminate my house but not enough to wake all of Santa Monica. The beach nine stories below is quiet, but the ocean outside my open, sliding-glass door roars.

There's no better time to sabotage a philandering surgeon's life.

I unlock my file cabinet and pull Rush's file. Cuddling around my coffee mug with my knees at my chest, I spread the documents out on the dining table in front of me.

With my limited understanding of Dr. Rush's job of cutting and sewing blood vessels, I can think of three ways to ruin his career. The crudest of which is to injure his hands and hope the damage is permanent. I sift through the documents Dr. Rush's wife gave me.

The bastard has hand insurance.

Even if he didn't, I'm more creative than that. Mutilating his hands is violent, which I'm against on principle unless I'm having a particularly bad day. Not to mention, my client asked me to destroy his career in such a way that he could watch it happen as a helpless bystander. I'm looking for something slower than amputating his arm from the wrist down, preferably with more theatrics.

An alternative would be to cause some sort of malpractice—for instance, tricking him into operating on the wrong side of the body. Think single mastectomy of a breast cancer patient's healthy breast. That's the type of dumbass error a doctor's reputation never shakes. Unfortunately, he's not a plastic surgeon or a surgical oncologist or any kind of doctor where that type of idiocy applies.

My medical knowledge is too limited to get him to slice into the wrong artery, and my conscience is too functional to let me tamper with the life of one of his patients. Which leaves me with framing him for violating some sort of physician law or rule. There's HIPPA, which forbids him from sharing any of his patients' personal or medical information. That'd be pretty easy with Rory's help. Leak a patient file. Leak a lot of patient files. Forge some texts from his cell or emails with HIPPA-protected data to someone outside of work. That's probably not the kind of career assassination my client is looking for, though.

I take a sip of my coffee and scan the Rushes' prenuptial agreement. It was signed eleven years ago, long before Rush had a salary of any kind and eight years before he started making six figures. What kind of gold digger did he think he was marrying? Did he think he'd proposed to a bomb that would tick for a decade before detonating? What moron would marry a medical student for the money he might make later? What if he failed? Or became a medical examiner for the police and made no money? What if he, God forbid, ended up working for a charity in a mosquito-ridden country with no toilets? Did he really think she was that shallow, that patient?

In California, the fact that Miles can't keep his dick in one vagina doesn't give Emory any advantage in the divorce. Even if she could establish residency in a state that would give her an advantage, the prenup allows for either party—in other words, Dr. Rush—to whore around without it affecting the division of the couple's assets. It was like he was planning to cheat and leave her penniless before he got down on one knee. So no, Miles didn't think Emory was waiting for an opportunity to take off with his money. He was waiting for his chance to.

I lean my elbows on the table and place my fingertips on my temples. Miles's life insurance policy is peeking out from under Reagan's Facebook screenshot. I slide it out to see how much he is worth dead. *Holy shit.* That's a lot of zeroes. Emory and her kids would be rich for a decade, or comfortable for two.

Huh.

Miles is a body. In fact, he's a white and safely upper-class body.

I pick up Reagan's Facebook profile. She's also white. Not upper class yet, but she's more or less a doctor. People value doctors. No one wants to see a good brain in bloody chunks outside its skull. Two doctors shot dead would be an outrage.

A waste.

A tragedy.

A hell of a good *tough-on-crime* ad.

I doubt I could get them to Xavier's In-n-Out in South Gate. But anyone can get in a hospital. Besides locked doors, they have minimal security. It's not impossible to sneak a gun in.

A black felon shooting two doctors at their place of work? Yeah, I think that's what Young had in mind. And Dr. Rush's three-million-dollar life insurance payout should satisfy the wife he betrayed with cold-dicked premeditation. And Rory and I will never hear about those silly embezzlement charges again.

And my dad will finally be a free man.

My bedroom door unlatches with Linus's voice following it. "Morning."

"Hey." I toss him a smile over my shoulder before I sweep the Rush documents back into the file. After they're securely tucked away, Linus buries a kiss in the skin below my ear and whispers, "You're up early."

I guide his hands to hug my waist from behind. "I gotta drive out to Lancaster before it's a hundred and twenty degrees."

"Drive? You can't drive."

I chuckle out a sarcastic, "Okay."

He pulls his face away from mine. "I'm serious. Your dad told me not to let you drive yourself anywhere."

"That was before I got arrested. It's fine now."

His forehead wrinkles as he studies me. "I'll take you."

"Linus—"

"What if you have another heart attack on the road?"

"I won't."

"What's in Lancaster?"

"My dad."

"Then I'm definitely coming with you."

"Why?"

"I owe him an apology."

"For what?"

"For leaving you."

Damn it. The white boy is so pretty when he talks about my dad. "Fine."

SEEING LINUS IN PRISON is like watching a puppy trying to walk in shoes. It's cute, but it's also like, *Who put shoes on the damn puppy? He's so uncomfortable and can't go where he needs to, and how is he going to pee if he can't lift his little paw?*

Huh. I hadn't noticed until now, but his face always has a puppy look, what with his big green eyes just a smidge too close together, a few strands of his golden-retriever hair straight and careless over his forehead, and his smile that says,

Are there down feathers all over the house from a torn-up pillow? Wasn't me. I've been over here just wagging my tail and looking so damn cute all day.

Linus stands behind me with no clue what to do with his arms or hands or eyes as I hug my dad, who, by the way, doesn't even acknowledge him before he sits down.

"Dad, really?"

"Oh." He pushes off the table. "He's with you?"

"Cal," Linus says as he reaches out his hand.

Dad's face hardens as he returns the obligatory handshake. Okay, so he isn't smitten by Linus's puppyness like I am.

Dad turns his attention to me before taking a seat again. "How you feeling, baby girl?"

I sit, inviting Linus to as well. He does, keeping his spine rigid and sweaty palms dry on his jeans.

"Much better."

Dad folds his hands on the table and tips his head Linus's direction. "What's that guy doing here? He's not staying with you anymore."

"I am, actually," Linus answers.

All right, the puppy shoes are coming off.

My dad, feigning deafness to Linus's voice, continues, "He left. You shouldn't tolerate anyone who treats you as less than the queen you are."

"Well, in his defense," I say with my hand on Linus's forearm, "I used him to ruin his father's career without his knowledge."

"Why would you do that?"

"Because I was hired to."

"Did his father deserve it?"

In unison, Linus and I answer, "Yes."

"Did you get paid well?"

"Thirty grand."

"Good girl." Dad turns to Linus. "Do you feel entitled to a percentage of this money since you were an involuntary independent contractor?"

Involuntary independent contractor? Is that a euphemism for pawn?

Linus straightens up, his face betraying that he's just as thrown by this question as I am. "No, sir. I don't."

"Why are you staying with her?"

"Because I promised I would. I should have never left in the first place."

"Yeah, but you like her, right?"

Oh, God.

"You're not just staying out of obligation."

Dad!

"Yes, sir." Linus cracks a smile. "I like your daughter very much."

Well, yeah, what is he supposed to say to my scary-ass dad? *No, she repels me and the sex is terrible?*

"Did you apologize to her?"

"Yes, and I came here to apologize to you."

My dad opens his folded hands. "Well…"

Linus takes a deep breath. "I'm sorry that I left Estlyn when I told you I wouldn't. I know it will take time to earn your trust back, but I hope that I will. I have no intention of breaking a promise I make to either of you again."

My dad cocks his head and smirks. "What kind of promises are you making to my daughter?"

Well, this took an unfortunate turn. "Dad, I need to talk to you in private." I nod to Linus. "Could you—"

"Sure." He leans in to kiss my cheek. Before Linus leaves, he offers his hand one more time to my dad. "Nice to meet you, Mr. Hayes."

My dad takes his hand. "Don't hurt my little girl, understand?"

"Yes, sir."

Once we're alone, I mutter, "That could have gone worse."

My dad crosses his arms on the table, watching Linus walk away. "He's white."

"*Is* he?" My lips purse as I pretend to contemplate Linus's race. "Well, shit. That explains why his penis is so small."

"God," Dad says as he runs his hands over his face. "I didn't need to know that."

I let out a quiet cackle. "Dad, I'm joking. I'm pretty sure it's just above average size."

"*Dillon!*"

Elbow on the table, I point at him. "That's

what you get for calling Cal to check on me. How invasive is that? I'm a grown-ass woman."

"You weren't acting like yourself. What if someone were holding you hostage or something?"

"Oh…" I hold my finger in front of him. "*Hell* no. Don't pretend like that is the first time you've done something like that."

"What are you talking about?"

"You call Rory sometimes."

"Yeah," he shrugs, "on special occasions like his birthday or the Superbowl."

"And I know you call Dean all the time."

"Not *all* the time."

I shoot him a skeptical look.

My dad throws his hands up in surrender. "He's like the son I never had."

"How? You never see him."

"Exactly. We talk on the phone once a week, and I complain that he doesn't visit me enough. Son I never had."

"Once a week? What the hell do you two have in common?"

"You. Also he says he likes to call me because his Catholic parents aren't, quote, 'as accepting as that new pope what's-his-name.' Dil, the boy needs a father figure."

"Fine," I groan. "Just don't call Cal, okay?

"No promises."

"Dad—"

"How'd you meet?"

I sigh and relent. "In a bar."

"The one he works at?"

"Yep."

"Why him?"

"He finished the E. E. Cummings poem I left him."

He sits back and nods, impressed. "Smooth."

"And I figured he was less likely to get shot at a traffic stop, so I could get attached." I reach my hands out in defense. "Not that I'm getting attached. Just saying… if it ever came to that."

My dad shoots me a crooked grin and nods. "What makes him worthy of you?"

I rest my head in my fingers as I think for a minute. My dad was like this with Michael, too—with every boy I ever liked. *Never once think that you aren't good enough for some boy. You're too good for all of them, baby girl. The right one has to prove he's worth your time.*

I click my tongue when I have an answer that will satisfy my dad. "He built me a reading tent."

"All right then." His shoulders relax as he cuts off his interrogation. "You wanted to talk about something?"

"Um, yeah." I wince. "It's about Mom."

"Okay." He shrugs. "What about her?"

"Did you, uh…" I take a deep breath and run my hands up and down my arms. "Do you feel, I don't know, guilty about what happened?"

"About killing her?"

I nod.

His eyes soften until they gloss with moisture. "Of course."

No, no, no, no, no. That's not the answer I was hoping for. Maybe I can get a different one. "Why? I mean, it was an accident. It was instinct. You did the right thing, it just had the wrong result."

"But I still took someone's life. That's not something I can give back."

"Okay," I mumble. "Do you regret it, though?"

"Yeah, that's what I'm saying. Forget about your mom. Dil, I took everything from you in that moment. I took away both your parents. I put you in another abusive home, even if unintentionally. And I ruined any chance you could have had to face your abuser in court."

Only my dad could take himself defending his only daughter and twist it into something he should be ashamed of. "But what if it hadn't gone that way?" I ask. "What if you'd had a guarantee that something good would come from killing her? Like, you were sure you'd be acquitted, we'd live together, and she'd never hurt me again?"

"No. Not even then. Killing someone isn't a justifiable means to an end."

"Never? Not any end?"

"Well..." He tips his head from side to side as he thinks. "Okay, so self-defense is acceptable, right? What else?" He asks the question like he's the teacher and I'm his student, even though he hasn't been in the classroom in almost fifteen years.

"Defense of the vulnerable."

"Right."

"War."

"Sure, but..." He gestures with his hands on the table, pointing and dividing an invisible illustration on its surface. "Even in those instances, even in those times where it very well may be necessary to take one life to save another, someone has to decide which one is worth saving and which isn't. I don't trust anyone enough to make that kind of decision, do you?"

I swallow over the thickness in my throat. "No, I don't."

"Look, I don't want you to think I regret throwing her off you, because—"

A weak smile lifts my lips. "I don't think that."

"I'm just saying violence is a last resort because it usually means humans deciding the value of other humans. That has yet to lead to anything good. There isn't one war that started without someone saying, 'Hey, we're better than those people over there.' Hemingway fought in War World I, and even he said, 'Never think that war, no matter how necessary, nor—'"

"'—how justified, is not a crime.'" I finish the sentence for my dad, the pacifist in prison for murder. "Wasn't Hemingway just an ambulance driver?"

My dad waves me off. "Baby girl, you know what it's like to have someone decide your value is less than theirs." And decide that about Michael.

My eyes watch my fingers fidgeting on the table. "Yeah."

"Is something bothering you? Why are you asking all this?"

"I just..." My eyes finally brave his. "I just never asked how you felt about it."

"You sure everything's all right?" He leans in and whispers, "Dil, whatever happened with..." Dad takes a deep breath, then releases it. "Did he ever find out?"

I force a smirk, as if that will convince him the situation with Monroe hasn't escalated from a campfire I tried to ignore to a wildfire covering thousands of acres. In a drought. With Santa Ana winds. And triple-digit highs. "No, and he won't."

He squints when he studies me. "Are you sure?"

I nod enough times to destroy my credibility, but he pretends to buy it anyway. "Yeah, Dad. You don't need to worry."

SEVENTEEN

Estlyn

Eleven Days Prior

Young thinks I am either incompetent or untrustworthy. One is accurate, the other ludicrous and offensive. No matter his reason, he is risking a third and, hopefully, final meeting with me.

It's after dark when I arrive at his campaign command center, which is a previously unoccupied storefront at a strip mall in Glendale. I fit in well with the buzz in the room—the copy machine whirring, poll number talk, phones ringing, and televisions humming with those obnoxious political ads.

"Can I help you?" a young blonde thing asks from her desk.

Okay, so I guess I don't blend in well. It probably has to do with my clueless wandering around the massive room.

"I have a meeting with Young."

"Your name?"

"Estlyn Collins."

She clicks on her computer and shakes her head. "I don't have you in his schedule."

"Ms. Collins, good to see you," Young announces as he strides toward me. His hand warmly welcomes mine, accompanied by that smile that is as fake as the veneers that comprise it. As he leads me to his back offices, he keeps up the facade. "Can I get you anything? Water? Dinner? We have some leftover—"

"I'm fine."

"I'll need you to leave your phone in the hall, for obvious reasons." Right. Because I want to have what I'm about to say recorded.

He shuts the two of us into his windowless office, decorated with a whiteboard and corkboard, doubling as a storage room for *Young for Governor* lawn signs—nothing like the almost-glamour of his downtown office.

Young leans back in his squeaky, not-made-of-leather chair, which is a shame because I like making cow-slaughtering jokes to myself at his expense. He scratches his salt-and-pepper sideburns as he starts, "So we need to talk about this allowance you're asking for."

"Well, we wouldn't have to if you hadn't planted heroin in my apartment and confiscated my assets. But, yes, it's hard to do a job with no money."

"I told you, we can't pay you."

No denial? *So you did plant those drugs, motherfucker.* This moment isn't as satisfying as I had hoped it would be. Probably because I'm still under his clammy thumb.

"The money isn't for me."

"What's it for?"

"It's a bribe."

"A hundred thousand dollars? Who the hell are you bribing?"

"In-n-Out employees don't just up and shoot doctors."

"So you're bribing Freeman to kill—"

"Would you like to guess some more, or should I just explain?"

He nods.

I sit up and clasp my hands in my lap. "Xavier has a thirteen-year-old son, Jayden, who he reunited with after he was released from prison. Jayden has cystic fibrosis and is on the waiting list for a lung transplant. Xavier is a match for donation, but, unfortunately for all parties, he's still using those lungs. Even if he wasn't and a healthy donor died in a motorcycle accident—"

"The surgery is expensive."

"Right. So, I will reach out to Xavier with the name of two doctors he needs to shoot in the UCLA Medical Center parking lot before he turns the gun on himself. Someone in the hospital will hear the *bang-bang*." I squint toward the ceiling before I add, "*Bang*. They will take him inside the hospital, check his ID, and see he's an organ donor. I will personally call his family—from a burner, obviously—to make sure his son will make a timely arrival at the hospital for the transplant. We will pay the family in cash, or, if you rather, we can do a wire transfer from an offshore account. My tech guy is a lot better at his job now than he was when he was nineteen."

His lips twist into a slimy smile at the mention of our embezzlement.

"Either way, Jayden will have his new lungs, and you will have your two upper-class, white bodies in a grotesque murder scene created by a felon Sellards acquitted." Arching my eyebrow, I cock my head and conclude, "I assume this meets your Willie Horton standards?"

His fingers tent at his fingertips again, in that evil not-so-genius way. "Who are the doctors?"

Swallowing past the narrowing in my throat, I pretend I'm not bothered by giving these people names pre-slaughter. "Miles Rush and Reagan Wathen."

"How'd you pick them?"

"Does it matter?" *Why are you insisting on seeing my cards?*

"Does your freedom?"

I huff and prop my head in my hands, massaging the tension from my scalp. "It makes another case of mine easier."

He nods. "And who's providing this gun?"

"If Xavier does not have access to a firearm…" Sucking in a breath, I exhale the words, "I have a guy who can sell me an unlicensed one."

"What's his name?"

I shake my head. "You're not arresting him after this."

"Why a hundred grand?"

"Because I'm not sure I can convince him to commit a double-murder-suicide for less."

"You'll have the money when you need it."

We stand, and he offers his hand again. This time, I don't shake it.

EIGHTEEN

Estlyn

TEN DAYS PRIOR

AMBUSHING PEOPLE IN THEIR workplace never gets old. The thrill of waiting in their office for their arrival or sitting at the restaurant where they meet clients or in their trailer on a movie set—it fills me with those same nerves I get before a date mixed with that swell of superiority subpoena-delivery boys must feel when they tell people they're getting sued.

This time, my toes bounce against the floor of a less-than-luxurious law office waiting room. And it's not my target's office. It's the office of the guy I turned down for a second date. And a "nightcap." And I'm about to ask him to do me another favor.

"I'm sorry, he's not in the rest of the day," Quin's assistant tells me from behind her computer.

I lean against the high portion of her desk. "Where is he?"

"I'm not supposed to say."

My eyes narrow before I tip my chin at her. "What's your name?"

She sits a little straighter and replies, "Miranda."

"You like your job here?"

Her young blue eyes dance with nerves. "Yes."

"They pay you well?"

"Pretty well."

"Working for a DDA, that's gotta look good on a résumé. What do you want to do after this?"

"Law school."

"And after that?"

"I—I don't know."

"Well, Miranda, if you want to keep your job, which will lead to law school, which will lead to this"—I twirl my finger through the air—"amorphous dream of yours, I recommend you tell me where Quinton is because I'll be happy to inform him *you* were the reason he missed the opportunity to see me today."

Shrinking back in her chair, she glances at the computer. "He's having lunch at Winsome."

"Is he with anyone?"

"His mom."

I pinch my smile between my teeth, then tap my hand on her desk. "Thank you, Miranda." I sling my messenger bag over my shoulder and, before leaving, wave my finger between us. "If you're going to make it in law school, you shouldn't let people push you around like this. Grow a nut, sweetie."

I make to Winsome before Quin and his mom are done with their soup and salad, respectively. This could not be more perfect. Quin loves his momma. He would never misbehave in front of her.

Without a word, I slide into the booth next to him and take a sip of his soda. Gross, Diet Coke. Isn't he a grown-ass man? "Have you tried the grilled cheese here?" I ask. "It's incredible."

"Dillon, what—"

I reach my hand across the table. "Mrs. Cunningham? I'm Dillon."

She takes my hand. "Pleasure?"

"I know your time with your son is precious, I mean, look at him." I pinch his cheek like I would never do to a baby because people don't like that. "He's adorable. But would you mind if I take just ninety seconds of your time together, starting now?" I set my phone with the stopwatch running on the table, then take Quin's hand.

"What the hell, Dil?" he growls as I drag him away. For a guy who's wanted to get in my pants for so long, he's awfully reluctant to follow me into the women's bathroom.

I push open the door. Two stalls. Damn it. I slam the first door in, but the second is locked. "Look, Quin, I know you might be a little sore about the whole boyfriend thing, but—" I knock on the closed stall. "Are you about done in there?"

There's a flush, followed by a miffed millennial opening the door.

"May we have the room?"

She surrenders it after a scoff and a quick wash of her hands.

After the door shuts, I turn back to Quin. "You want to be DA?"

"What?"

"Do you want to be the Los Angeles County DA?"

"Well, yeah, eventually I'll run for it, but right now—"

"Do you want a guarantee?"

"You can't guarantee—"

"Quin, do you want something pretty damn close?"

He crosses his arms and sits back against the edge of the counter. "You can offer me that?"

"Yes, I just need your help."

"Really? I'm *shocked*."

I point at his chest. "And you need mine."

He cackles. "I do?"

"You're introducing Young at his campaign fundraiser, right? The one at The Majestic Downtown?"

"Yeah, how did you—"

"I know everything," I snap. "Which is how I know you're walking into a career assassination. Please, help me help you."

His hands rest on his belt. "What would kill my career?"

"I would."

"Is this a threat?"

"Does it need to be?"

"*Excuse* me?"

"Look, you can be collateral damage, or you can be a civic hero."

"Are those my only options?"

"Our ninety seconds are almost up. Which is it?"

"Hero, I guess." His conviction is truly moving.

"Meet me at Bentley's Dive in Culver City tonight at eight."

"Okay." After a long silence, which reminds us both we're in a restaurant bathroom, he adds, "Can I eat lunch with my mom now?"

"Oh, yeah." I nod and lead him out of the ladies' room.

NINETEEN

Cal

TEN DAYS PRIOR

"HEY, I DIDN'T THINK I'd get to see you until after work. What are you doing here?" I lean over the bar to kiss Estlyn, but she puts her finger over my lips.

"Are you giving Dean free drinks?"

I notice Elliot stops scooping ice out of the freezer drawer behind me, probably so he can hear my answer. "Of course not."

She hops up on a barstool and presses her elbows into the counter. Her chin cradled in her crisscrossed fingers, she raises an eyebrow. "Then I'd like to put my martini on his tab, please."

She holds my gaze tightly, waiting for me to give evidence of my lie in the silence. "Sure." I throw a smile her way before I turn to get her glass.

When I return to the bar, Estlyn's fingers slip between the buttons of my shirt. She pulls me close and opens my mouth with hers, her hands clutching at my chest and neck. She breathes in sharply through her nose and runs her fingers through my hair and down my back. God, is she going to start taking my clothes off right here?

An inch from my lips, she whispers, "You're so fucking pretty, Linus."

Pretty?

"Thanks…" I guess.

"You have eyes an Aussie puppy would envy."

I'm a pretty puppy? That's oddly the most genuine compliment I've ever received. I chuckle. "People tell me that all the time."

She shoves me back across the bar and sits down. "I have a meeting here."

So… no fucking on the bar? That's for sure not happening?

"Okay?"

"I'm answering your question. That prosecutor who took me out the other night? He's helping me with something."

Ah. So sex before last call is definitely out of the question. "Getting your stuff back?" I ask, trying not to sound disappointed at this turn of events.

"In the spirit of full disclosure, we're meeting here. In front of you. I know it might look like a date, but it's not. I told him I have a boyfriend."

I smirk. "Boyfriend?"

"Right. Elliot," she deadpans.

"What?" Elliot slides up next to me until

all the personal space between us is gone. The stench that infiltrated his apartment has latched onto his T-shirt as well. How he still manages to be such a slut I will never understand.

"Nothing." I wave him off before I seal the cocktail shaker.

"You know," he says to Estlyn with a thumb jutting in my direction, "I'm better in bed than him."

Maybe, but I'm a pretty puppy. Suck on that, Elliot.

Estlyn cringes. "How would you know? Did you... *watch*? Listen at the door? Conduct bedroom exit polls?"

"No, no, no," he laughs. "I'm just more experienced. And, well," he ogles her, "the response—in my *experience*—has been overwhelmingly positive."

"Congratulations." Estlyn shifts her weight to her elbow nearest him. "It's just, when I hear *experienced*, I think *herpes*."

I press my lips together to suppress my laughter.

"What?" he chuckles.

"Or chlamydia. Once in a while, I'll think of gonorrhea or HPV—you know, what you gain from 'experience.'"

"I don't have an STD."

"Have you been tested?"

"Well, no."

She whispers through a grimace, "Does it burn when you pee?"

"*What?*"

She lifts her right shoulder to her ear. "Yeah, I think I'll take my chances with less-experienced Linus. Might be fun to teach him a thing or two." She winks, then tips her chin, requesting I pass her the drink I made.

After a sip, she returns to our previous conversation. "Anyway, I know you just got cheated on, so I didn't want you to get all insecure and jealous when you saw me with another guy, especially when I'm looking so svelte in this dress." She stands and backs up enough for me to see the black material hugging her body. "See how itty bitty it is?"

"Yep." I nod. "Very sexy."

"Now," she takes her drink, "I'm going to walk away so you can guess what kind of underwear I'm wearing. I'll give you a hint." She cups a hand to the side of her mouth and whispers, "It's invisible."

I laugh out. "Did you start drinking before you got here?"

"No, but I took something called…" She pauses, struggling to recall and pronounce her next word. "Alprazolam at home."

I yank the drink from her hand, sloshing vermouth all over her arm. "You can't drink with Xanax."

"I didn't take Xanax. I took *Alprazolam*," she slurs.

"Is that what they prescribed you at the hospital for anxiety?"

She nods.

"That's Xanax. How many did you take?"

She pushes out her bottom lip and looks up. "Some, I want to say?"

"Some? How many is some? Three? Four?"

"Maybe?"

"Why?"

"I was *anxious*," she says with air quotes. "I'm supposed to take them when I'm"—air quotes—"*anxious*, so I don't have another"—air quotes—"*heart attack*."

Estlyn reaches for the drink, but I take it to the back counter. Even with my back to her, she keeps talking.

"I'm having a stressful week what with revenging and all, and Dean took away my poker night. How am I supposed to relax?"

"I didn't take it away," Dean interjects. When I turn around, I notice him and Rory striding up to the counter. "You got one of the players arrested. There isn't a game to return to." He points to the martini. "Is anyone going to drink that?"

I hand him Estlyn's drink amid her protests. "Dean, tell her she can't drink with Xanax."

He turns to Estlyn. "Bitch, you can't drink with your Xanax. There will be less alcohol for me." After swallowing a mouthful, he adds, "Prick Prosecutor was parking when we got here."

"Thanks," she says, sliding off the stool. Halfway to the door, she calls over her shoulder, "Guess you won't be seeing my invisible underwear tonight."

"As long as he won't be seeing them, either." I bury my face in my hands and mutter. "She's mildly stoned."

"Yeah, you'll still get lucky," Dean says as he tips Estlyn's martini to his lips.

"Beer?" I ask Rory.

"Might as well. Liv is mad at me anyway."

"Ready to try something cloudy and Belgian?"

Rory's face contorts like a child's choking down broccoli. "Gross."

"Corona?"

"Light."

"Why is Liv mad at you?" Dean asks.

"Oh, we're planning a barbecue with our families to tell them we're pregnant, and Estlyn won't go. Liv wants me to try to make her. I won't. You know, girl/family drama."

"Ah."

"Why won't she go?" I ask as I hand him his college-girl beer.

"Estlyn doesn't see our parents anymore."

"Yeah? Why?"

He takes a deep breath and winces. "They sort of took the cop's side after Michael died."

"Holy shit." I wouldn't see them anymore, either.

He nods before taking a swig of beer. "It's not like they thought Michael deserved to die, but they also didn't think the officer deserved to be charged since he was 'just doing his job' and 'protecting himself from an armed man.'"

"Jesus."

"Estlyn hasn't seen them since her dad's verdict, so," Rory squints as he thinks, "that was five years ago. They try to reach out to her, invite her to every Thanksgiving and Christmas, but she cut them off. She even paid them back for adopting her a few years back."

"What, like the fees? Or—"

"Yeah, plus the money they would have been paid if they'd fostered her those last two years she was a minor. I guess what they said made her think they never wanted her as their daughter. You know, made her feel like they were embarrassed by her skin and only took her because she and I were sort of a package deal."

I glance past Rory at Estlyn and Prosecuting Prick sliding into a booth together. "But she still has their last name."

"My last name."

My eyes snap to Rory's—muddy hazel, surrounded by freckled skin that looks nothing like Estlyn's. But he's her family. She chose him. She decided he would stay in her pack.

"She didn't want to take her mom's maiden name?"

Dean and Rory share a sideways glance.

"What? Are they not close, either?"

Rory shakes his head. "She's dead, and they wouldn't be if she were alive."

"Oh." My fingers tap on the bar as I swallow all this information. I'm with half her family now. I met the other half Saturday. That's all she has? Really?

Someone calls me from a few seats down. As I stretch for a bottle of scotch, I peek over the row of people at the bar. Estlyn's hovering over the table, talking with her not-date.

I keep an eye on her for the next hour or so, until I notice her cradling her forehead in both palms. When she doesn't lift her face after a few minutes, I round the bar and make my way to her, not sure if she's dozing off mid-conversation or nauseated and about to puke all over the floor.

Estlyn perks up once I make it to her side. "Linus, hi!" She snatches my arm and yanks me into the seat next to her. "Quin, this is Cal. He's my boyfriend. He writes movies."

"Really?" Quin cocks his head and gives me a once-over. "Because it looks like he's a bartender."

"Nice to meet you, too." Jackass.

Estlyn curls around my arm and leans her head on my shoulder. Out of nowhere, she chokes down a massive sob and cries, "I missed you."

I slip my arm behind her back and tuck her against my chest. "When?"

"When you were working."

"Twenty feet away?"

"Uh-huh," she sniffs.

"Okay. That's the Xanax."

Her bawling continues unhindered as her head slumps into my lap. "It's *Alprazolam.*"

I stroke her hair away from her face. "I know, Est. You're right."

"My head feels heavy."

"Is she okay?" Quin interjects. "Do I need to call 9-1-1 or something?"

My fingers slip to the pulse in her throat. "Can you breathe, Est?"

Her eyes flutter closed as she works to take a breath. "You smell like coconut rum."

I shake my head at Quin. This isn't the first benzo—that's the class of drug Xanax and its downer friends like Valium and Ativan fall into—overdose I've had to deal with, but it's not as bad as some of my mom's were. "Estlyn, I'm going to take you home, okay?"

"Okay," she mumbles, then crawls up me. Estlyn buries her face in my neck, slipping her knees on either side of my thighs.

"Yeah, I'm not going to take you home like this."

Her arms fall limp over my shoulders, head joining them.

"Est?"
Nothing.
"Guess I'm taking you home like this."

I BRUSH ESTLYN'S CAREFREE curls away from her clammy forehead. The breeze from the window cools her skin as her body tenses around her pillow.

"How're you feeling?"

She closes her eyes against my touch. Her breathing is shallow and slow into her pillowcase. "I think I read the label wrong," she mumbles.

God, I hope that's all that happened.

"My chest was hurting. I thought it would help."

I stroke her cheek with my thumb. "Does it still hurt?"

She shakes her head.

"Are you still dizzy?"

"Mm-hmm," she groans. Her fingers reach up to massage her temple. "It's not going to work without Quin."

"What's not?"

"I was worried he wouldn't help after I refused to show him my invisible underwear."

"Did he?"

"He's going to help."

"Get your stuff back?"

She shakes her head. "With a job."

"That's great, but, Est, you're supposed to be on leave. How many jobs are you working?"

The fingers at her forehead split and raise in answer. Two.

"Can you postpone one?"

"No."

"Can I do anything to help?"

A tear slips down her cheek, and she hugs a second pillow to her chest. "I don't feel good."

"I know, babe," I whisper.

I push her hair aside, so the heat of her skin can sink into my lips. I'm not sure I've ever been so confused or captivated by another person. For all her independence, for all the fear she inflicts on others, Estlyn is a fragile, intricate mess. Which isn't odd in and of itself. What's unique is her willingness to show it, the freedom she feels to break in front of me at night and the next morning scare the shit out of whomever she needs to. She clashes. She's a tug-of-war.

Estlyn is brave and Estlyn is afraid.

Estlyn is in command and Estlyn is losing control.

Estlyn is shattered and Estlyn is whole.

Estlyn is a child and Estlyn is a grown-ass woman.

Estlyn is brilliant and Estlyn doesn't know.

Estlyn has ghosts and Estlyn haunts others.

Estlyn is good.

Estlyn is bad.

Estlyn just is.

"Do you want to drink some water?"

She shakes her head.

"I'm going to hang on to those pills from now on, okay?"

Her eyes shoot open. "Linus, I didn't mean to take too many. I think it said take one up to three times a day, and I took three or something."

"I know. But my mom's an addict, so I'm really good at hiding pills." I smile, but she doesn't.

"When did you start doing that? For your mom?"

I recline on the mattress beside her and trail my hand to her waist. "My parents divorced when I was nine, so sometime after that."

"You lived with her?"

I nod. "Well, until I was twelve. The courts gave my dad custody after she got pulled over drunk driving with my sister and me in the car."

"You have a sister?"

I nod.

"Older or younger?"

"Younger."

"Thank God you're okay." She exhales.

I shrug. "Mom was drunk most of the time. She drove pretty well even then."

"Well, apparently not." Estlyn lets out a weak laugh. "You ever see her?"

"She's in San Diego now, so I don't see her as

often as I'd like to."

"You should. Girls like boys who make an effort with their moms."

I caress her hips and waist through her thin tee until her hand finds mine. "Good to know."

"You liked living with her better than with your dad?"

"Yeah."

"They took me away from my favorite parent, too."

"Shit deal, isn't it?"

She nods and takes a labored breath. "Can I ask you something?"

"Of course."

"My dad—why did you care about impressing him the other day?"

"What do you mean?"

"He's in prison for murder."

My lungs release a nervous chuckle. "I know."

"I mean, why were you trying so hard?"

"Well, because he's your dad. *You* love him. You care what he thinks. So I care, too."

"You don't think killing someone makes him," she works hard to fill her lungs, "an animal? You know, less than human?"

"Of course not."

Her fingers crawl up my chest, then slip down my torso. She tugs her body closer to mine and says, "He didn't murder her."

Her? "Okay."

"He killed her, but it was an accident. But if it hadn't been an accident—"

"Then he'd still be your dad." I barely see her dark eyes rise to mine in the faint light from the open window, but it's not so dark that I can't see the dread in them. "Are you okay?"

She answers by nuzzling her face in my chest. Her lungs fight against the medication to inhale the scent of my skin. I pull the covers up around us and rest my cheek against her hair. My eyes stay open until I'm sure she's fallen asleep. After she does, I read on my phone so I can listen for her breath, so I can hear if the drug stops it. It hasn't by the time I doze off around three.

TWENTY

Cal

Eight Days Prior

I WALKED IN AT the wrong time.

They've all seen me, so it's not like I can slide back out Estlyn's door to avoid the touchable tension filling her apartment.

Rory's arms are crossed. Some olive-skinned woman I've never seen before is catching her breath after yelling. And Estlyn is clad in reading glasses at the dining table, working away on her laptop. From the few seconds I've been here, I gather she's stonewalling whatever argument the other two are trying to drag her into.

I clear my throat. "Is this a bad time?"

Without looking up from her computer, Estlyn responds by pointing back and forth between me and the teary-eyed brunette. "Linus, this is Olivia. Olivia, that's Cal."

Ah.

Yeah, I want no part in what I assume is the *Should Estlyn reconcile with her adoptive parents for the sake of her unborn niece or nephew?* fight. I'd have to take Estlyn's side to be loyal to my temporary girlfriend, but I'm not exactly keen on contributing to a pregnant lady's tears. Also, Estlyn is a hard-ass. She could make a serial killer cry without my help.

I'm still between the back of the couch and the kitchen—in other words, just inches inside the apartment—when Olivia nod-glares a thanks-for-interrupting greeting my way and resumes castigating Estlyn.

"It has been five fucking years, Dillon! You're not doing this because you're hurt. You're doing this because you're stubborn and going to this party would be admitting defeat in whatever war you're trying to win. But you're the only one fighting! You're the only one who cares anymore."

Estlyn takes a sip of her wine, still focused on the laptop in front of her. "I am," she agrees. Her answer is cold, not heated like Olivia's, and her following silence is terrifying—like, sociopath scary. Or maybe she's going all Muhammed Ali on her, letting Olivia wear herself out beating the shit out of her. Once she's tired, Estlyn will knock her out.

"You're what?" That's Olivia.

"The only one who cares anymore."

"It's a stupid grudge. They apologized." She waves her hand at me and adds, "And you've obviously moved on."

Oh, shit.

That is the last jab Estlyn's going to take. It's gotta be. Her eyes shut a moment, her breath pulling in at the sting of Olivia's words. I wait for her reply, but she has none. Instead, she raises her wine glass to her lips again—not for a sip, for a gulp.

What the hell am I supposed to do here? My eyes meet Rory's for any nonverbal advice he can offer. With a slight shake of his head, he entreats me to be silent.

Estlyn's shoulders relax as she returns her glass to the table. It's as if she can't lift her eyes at all, not that she is refusing to like before. "You familiar with the Fitzgeralds, Olivia?"

I'm not sure what this has to do with anything, but Olivia would be smart not to answer her. Because Estlyn and her English degree know where this is heading, and I don't think Olivia is going to be able to get off the mat once we all get there.

"Who?" Olivia asks.

"Zelda and Scott." She sheds her glasses and glances Olivia's way for a moment. "The twentieth-century writers. Anyway, their love letters to each other are published. In one of them, Zelda wrote, 'Thanks again for saving me. Someday, I'll save you, too.'" Estlyn's throat rolls before she adds, "Scott died eight years before Zelda. I've always wondered if she got a chance to save him."

Estlyn's gaze falls with the volume of her voice. "It's hard to describe those few seconds between life and death, those seconds when I knew that I couldn't do anything to save Michael." Her eyes squeeze shut, and she shakes her head. "It was just this barrage of 'What do I say?' and 'What do I do?' You know, do I tell him everything I want him to know before he dies, or will that make him lose any hope he has left of living? Do I try, I mean really try, to stop the bleeding so he doesn't think I've given up on him? Or do I force myself to accept it and do my best to be calm so he can have peace in those last moments of existence, knowing he did, in fact, save me?"

Estlyn takes a deep breath. "'Whatever happens now, whatever happens after this, you and I will still be.' That's what I wish I had said to him." She glances back at Olivia. "No, I haven't moved on. I'm not over it. Because I didn't get to save him. The least I can do is refuse to tolerate people who treat Michael like shit. So, please, stop wasting your energy and my time."

Olivia's lips part, but she thinks better of responding. Either that or she has no answer. *Don't feel bad, Liv. Estlyn does that to people. I wouldn't know what to say, either.* But I also wouldn't have said something so stupid to begin with. I've known Estlyn less than a month, and even I know better than to ever say she's over Michael.

The silence feels as heavy as lead, but, before it has time to crush us, the door behind me opens. Our heads all turn as Dean bursts into the room shouting, "If y'all are fornicating, I'm here and will have my earbuds out in three, two—Oh, hey, guys!"

I don't get it. Why is he *always* here? Does Dean have obnoxious roommates or a cockroach infestation? How does he have such impeccable instinct about the worst time to pop through the door?

"Don't let me interrupt this domestic dispute," he says after a quick read of the room. He rounds the kitchen counter to the refrigerator, adding, "I'm just here for the *HBO*."

There it is. HBO.

He peeks up from the open fridge. "Cal, have you seen Sharp Objects? Creepy as fuck. I'll rewatch the first episode with you if you haven't seen it." Disappearing into the fridge again, he adds, "I know. I'm *that* good a friend. What the hell? Where's the beer?"

"You drank it all, Dean," Estlyn snaps. "And you never left the twenty you promised."

After he shuts the fridge, he starts to dig through the cabinet beside it. "Rory helped." Olivia's livid green eyes flicker just as Dean catches his mistake. "I mean, uh, Cal helped."

"I thought Cal didn't drink?"

How does Olivia know that?

Dean shrugs and closes the cabinet, his arms

full of health store junk food. "You're on your own, Ror." To me, he nods toward the couch. "Come on! Murdered girls with missing teeth."

What the hell kind of cloth are Estlyn and he cut from? Doesn't matter. I gladly take advantage of the life preserver Dean is throwing me, because he sure as hell isn't chucking one Rory's way.

My ass is just about to hit the couch when Olivia whisks behind me and slams her way out the door. I turn to Dean and make the *Yikes, should we be here?* pained smile. Dean answers with a *Yes, there's HBO* shrug and turns on the TV.

"God, Dillon, you gotta stop these Olympic-level guilt trips."

Whoa. Girl Beer is standing up to Estlyn? I've only ever seen Dean do that. I want to watch. I shouldn't watch. *Don't turn around. Don't turn around.*

"Guilt trips?"

I glance over my shoulder at Estlyn as she replies. I'm weak. I know.

"My Olympic sport is lying."

"You know what Olivia's trying to do, right?"

"Make the world perfect for her vaginal excrement?"

"She's trying to give me a family, you know, because some of us don't have birth families anymore."

Leaning back in her chair, Estlyn crosses her

arms. "I thought you said *I* had the gold medal in guilt trips."

"This isn't about you!" Rory yells with his hands flying in the air. "Look, I'm sorry that Michael died and I'm sorry our parents were shitty about it back then, but do you know all the shitty things you do that people forgive you for?"

With a raised finger, she challenges, "Name one thing I've done that's as shitty as what they said."

Dean drapes his arm over the back of the couch and chimes in, "You told me that I would die alone, unloved even by the soil my rotting body would nourish." He returns his attention to the TV. "And I'm over it."

Estlyn rolls her eyes. "Clearly."

"In ninth grade," Rory interjects, "you told Jamie Forster that I jacked off to *The Notebook* when you *knew* I liked her!"

Yeah, I really shouldn't be here. Will anyone notice if I duck out the door? Or hide in the bathroom? Or jump off the balcony?

"I was trying to help you! I thought it'd make you look cute or sweet or something. Girls eat that shit up."

"Well, she didn't. And I wasn't jacking off to it!"

"Then what did I walk in on?"

"Should've said *A Walk to Remember*," Dean interrupts with his mouth full.

"No…" Estlyn shakes her head. "That would be bordering necrophilia."

"But it makes him seem sensitive. Sends the message, 'I'll love you even if you die young. Or look like you're dying when you don't wear makeup.'"

"Yeah," she purses her lips and tilts her head in consideration. "Yeah, I guess you're right."

"There was nothing else on TV!" Rory shouts.

His last word echoes in the apartment until it fades to a silence so vibrant, I'm forced to acknowledge it. When I finally turn toward the fight in the dining room, I realize all three of them are waiting for me to air out my grievance with Estlyn.

Yep, should have jumped off the balcony when I had the chance.

"Well?" Estlyn prompts me.

This feels like a trap, so much so that I say, "This feels like a trap."

"Ooh…" Dean gushes, "new guy has something to say!"

Seriously, why the hell does he have a key?

Bouncing on the couch, Dean pleads, "Tell us! Tell us!"

I clear my throat and, just above a whisper, say, "You told your dad I have a small penis."

Dean chuckles. Rory cringes. Estlyn stands.

"One," she says with a finger in the air, "I was joking. And two," she raises another finger, "you weren't supposed to hear that."

"Yeah, I think your penis is ample enough for her," Dean says. "I *heard*."

Yeah, Dean. I remember.

"Just..." Rory sighs, "don't be a dick, Dillon." He walks toward the entrance, murmuring "See ya, guys" as he passes behind us and disappears out the door.

"I still think mine's the worst," Dean announces as he presses Play.

Estlyn scoots her chair in with her hip, drinking wine from a glass in one hand and flipping Dean off with the other.

"You don't have any whiskey or scotch?" Dean calls to her as she wanders out of the room.

"Scotch?" Estlyn says. "Are you an old, straight man?"

"If I were, would you have my baby?" He dances his eyebrows up and down at me like I'm going to appreciate that comment.

"I have wine. BYOB next time," she calls from the kitchen. Estlyn's still in there when she hollers, "Your dick is fabulous, Linus." Reemerging with two wine glasses pinched between her fingers and a chilled bottle in her other hand, she joins us in the living room, setting everything on the coffee table. "If you don't believe me," she says as she pours wine into one of the glasses, "I'd be happy to prove it to you."

Dean tosses his hands in the air. "Bitch, move

out of the way. I can't see the TV."

"You don't live here." She nods to the chaise before climbing around us to recline there. "Linus, cuddle me. I'm tired."

I snicker, but it somehow ends up sounding more like a giggle—a masculine one, though. "Are you going to say *please*?"

She flops back onto the couch. "Do I need to?"

Dean nods and whispers, "Good job. Consistency is important with toddlers."

Estlyn glares at me. "*Please*, Linus, cuddle me, and I might do things to you under this blanket."

"Dean's here."

"Fine. I won't do anything too good under the blanket."

Dean hasn't flinched. He's engrossed in his show.

I shrug and slide to the corner with my arm open to her. Estlyn throws the blanket over us before she sinks into my side and shuts her eyes.

So many scenes in the show pass before she says anything that I think she's out.

"Linus?" she finally whispers.

Maybe I'm not as good at getting her to fall asleep as I thought.

"Yeah?"

"I like you."

I smile and blush high-school style when I look down at her. "I like you, too, Estlyn."

Her fingers take the fabric of my shirt and rub it between them. "I love Michael."

"I know, babe."

"Can you live with that?"

It's a simple question, but it requires more than a trite answer. Estlyn doesn't want a yes if I can tolerate her missing Michael. She's not even asking if I'm willing to comfort her in her indefinite grief. She's telling me her love for Michael will never fade, and her feelings for me may never compare. She wants to know, if that's the case, whether I still think she's worth it.

I wrap both arms around the slender body she's only ever entrusted to one other person. "Of course." I bury my lips in her hair and whisper, "I'm sorry."

She nods—what she does when she can't say anymore.

TWENTY-ONE

Cal

SEVEN DAYS PRIOR

"OKAY, SO HE DECIDED he does want you to cut the narration in your second draft," Whitney says from behind her desk.

"Sure."

She rocks back in her rolling chair and asks, "What do you think about asides?"

My tongue presses into the cheek of my smirk. "I'd be happy to give them a try."

"Great." She smiles and leans forward to hand me my writer's contract. "They agreed to two hundred against four hundred."

Hell yes. I sign and initial, then give it back.

"They gave me the check for your first fifty since we turned in your draft last week," she says as she passes me the envelope with my cut in it.

I want to rip into the envelope. I want to stand on the chair and sing, *I'm getting paid to write again! I can do more than just get people drunk!* I want to do that thing actors do in musicals where they put their foot on the back of the chair, tip it to the ground, and land gracefully with arms outstretched. I could add a chorus of, *Suck it, you hairy-ass son of a bitch. Suck it, suck it, suck it!* But I feel that would be less satisfying in front of my new agent than it would be directly in front of my dad. Maybe I could go to his set after I cash the check and then make it rain on myself while doing the chair/singing thing in a swirl of fluttering Franklins.

After I get back Estlyn's ring, of course.

I don't involve Dean this time. I can't risk him forcing another nineties' romantic comedy on me. Nothing is worth that.

Wyatt, who, to my disappointment, has not grown a mustache since I *last* saw him, is at his desk when I show up with a stack of one-hundred-dollar bills in a fat manila envelope. I've never been so anxious to pass off a parcel in my life. I'm not capable of being inconspicuous enough to carry around this much cash. You have to have the smoothness caliber of one of the *Ocean's Eleven* crew to avoid leaving sweaty palm prints on the golden paper, and based on the way this envelope looks, I'd never make the casino-robbing cut.

"Detective Kelly?"

He looks up at me with tilted curiosity. "Dean's friend?"

Nope, that is not what I want to go by. "Cal.

I'm here for Dillon Collins's ring."

"Right," he nods. He directs me to sit in the chair in front of his desk before turning to search his computer. His eyebrows knit together before he types again. "Dillon Collins, right?"

"Yeah. But it could be under Dillon Hayes."

"No, the record of the civil forfeiture is definitely under Collins. But..." His pause is filled with *click-clacking* on the keyboard. "They already turned the property over to the DEA."

"That can't be right. I thought you said I had three weeks. That was a week ago."

"Usually she would have thirty days to file a claim, but..." More clicking. More clacking. "Huh. ADA Ramirez authorized an exception."

What the fuck? "So, it's just gone? Her ring is lost somewhere with the DEA? Where is that even?"

He sighs. "There's one off the 101. You'll take the Alameda exit."

What am I supposed to do with directions, drive over to the Drug Enforcement Agency and demand they sell me her ring? "Yeah, but is it there?" I'd like to know before I show up at the DEA with eighteen grand in cash.

Wyatt shakes his head. "I don't know. Hang on." He picks up the phone. "I have a buddy there." After a moment, he says, "Yeah, can I speak to Agent Thurston?" Another moment. "Thurston, it's Kelly. Did we turn over a civil forfeiture to you guys on Friday?" More moments. A nod. "Did it include a diamond ring?" Two more moments. "Do you still have it?" One last moment. No, it's more like an hour. "Okay, thanks." He hangs up.

"What'd he say?"

"They sold it."

TWENTY-TWO

Estlyn

SEVEN DAYS PRIOR

I FIGURE THREE O'CLOCK is the ideal time to do this. It's after the lunch rush, before the dinner rush, and will land me squarely in rush-hour traffic, which will give me enough time to turn back into Linus-friendly Estlyn before I see him at home. I'm not sure he'd be as enamored with murder-plotting Estlyn.

I stand in line at In-n-Out with only two people in front of me and one person at the register. It's not Xavier, but I saw him pass behind the girl taking orders a moment ago.

"Hi, what can I get for you?" the short, Hispanic twenty-something asks from behind the counter.

"Yeah, could I speak to the manager?" Then I whip my credit card in front of me. "And get some fries and a strawberry milkshake?"

Xavier shoots me a polite grin a few moments later when he approaches the counter. "Hi, you wanted to speak to a manager?"

I force a smile. "Actually, I wanted to speak to you, Xavier. Do you have a moment?"

A smirk slides up his right cheek. Oops. He thinks I'm hitting on him? He's in for a crushing disappointment. "Anything you need."

"Order number forty-seven!" another employee shouts, sliding my fries and shake onto the counter. I take them and nod my head toward a booth. He pushes through the half door to follow me.

Xavier sits down, takes off his paper In-n-Out hat, and runs his hands over his buzz cut. I slide my fries over the table to him, but he puts his hands out to decline.

"Xavier Freeman, correct?" I ask as I pop the lid off my milkshake.

His expression morphs from flattered to creeped. "Yes."

I dunk two crisp fries in the pink ice cream. "You have a son, Jayden, with CF?"

Xavier grimaces either at my knowledge of his ill son or at my shoveling milkshake-covered fries into my mouth. I can't tell. "Why?"

"He lives with his mother, Jasmine Brown, in Downey?"

His hands slap the table. "Okay, who the fuck are you?"

"My name is Estlyn Collins. I've been hired to destroy your life."

"What the hell? Why? By who?"

"Whom. And you know how it is being that black guy always in the wrong place at the wrong time?" I point to him. "Congratulations, that's you."

He pushes up from the table, but before he can walk away I say, "I'll give you a hundred grand." Xavier pauses, his fingertips glued to the table. "Jayden needs that. If you walk away now, you'll never forgive yourself for what you didn't do for him."

He drops back into the booth. "I'm listening."

TWENTY-THREE

Cal

SEVEN DAYS PRIOR

UNFORTUNATELY, I HAVE TO involve Dean this time. Since we won't be seeing Wyatt, I think we can avoid a Rupert Everett rerun. Unless forcing him to accompany me to look at engagement rings will make him think of weddings and how he doesn't have one in the near future because he no longer has Wyatt in his life because he's afraid of commitment.

No. That's on him.

"You remember what it looks like, right?"

Dean wrinkles his lips to the left as he looks in the ring case. We're in this jewelry resale store in Beverly Hills. It's the place the DEA sold it to, but apparently everyone is calling off their engagements and getting divorced because there are a shit-ton of rings here. "It was a diamond."

That narrows it down.

He taps on the glass. "*Maybe* that one. Excuse me?" He lifts his face to the one girl working here. "When did you get this one?"

"Which one?"

"The diamond one with the circle of little diamonds around it."

She shrugs.

"What's the newest one you guys have gotten?"

"I don't know."

Dean straightens up with his fists on his hips. "Do you have a manager?"

"He's on vacation."

Dean presses his hands into the top of the glass and scans the rings. "Cal, can't you just bring her here? She'll know which one."

"No, because then it won't be a surprise."

He smirks at me. Yep, that sounded bad. I'm going to surprise my new girlfriend with an engagement ring from her dead boyfriend? "I—I mean, she'd try to pay for it then. And this is something I don't think she should pay for." I tap on the glass to try to draw his attention away from the fact I insist on buying Estlyn a ring.

Dean scans the jewelry again. "Was it a Tiffany?" he mutters. Then to the not-working employee, "Are any of these Tiffany's?"

She peers into the case. "Yeah, actually."

Dean arches an eyebrow at her. "You know something?"

She rolls her eyes and unlocks the case from the back. Reaching in, she pulls out a ring showcased on its own finger-shaped display. Shit, that's definitely an eighteen-grand diamond. There are even diamonds on the band.

Again, well done, Michael, I think. If this is, in fact, the ring he picked out for her.

"Is that the one?" I ask Dean.

His lips push up and eyebrows scrunch as he studies it. "I want to say yes."

"You want to?"

"Hey, I've only seen it, like, once, and that was years ago!"

"What's the price of this one?" I ask the sort-of-working employee.

"$19,995."

I drop the heavy envelop on the glass. "I'll give you eighteen in cash right now for it."

"Eh..." she winces as she hesitates. "I don't think I'm supposed to haggle."

Dean leans on the display case, his fingers' proximity to the ring and his face's proximity to the girl's both making her visibly uneasy. "Honey, this is a yuppie pawn shop. You haggle."

I jump in to rescue the intimidated salesgirl. "What's your commission rate?"

"Twenty percent."

"Do you know what twenty percent of eighteen thousand is?"

"Uh," she crosses her arms, "thirty-six hundred?"

I nod. "Do you know what twenty percent of

zero is?"

With a defeated exhale, she releases her arms and nods toward the register.

Dean slaps me on the shoulder. "You're welcome."

There isn't a single viral video of a guy giving a girl her dead boyfriend's engagement ring. No video at all, actually.

I checked.

Since there is no precedent for not proposing to a temporary girlfriend with a diamond ring she already owned, I'm forced to wing it. I realize this isn't as big a deal as popping the question or even asking her to be my permanent girlfriend, but it feels significant enough to require some sort of fanfare. The problem is, it's not my ring to give.

And I'm not Michael.

When I open the door to her empty apartment, I'm faced with just how not-Michael I am. I slip off my shoes and run my fingers over the charcoal fabric on the back of the couch. Estlyn mentioned she and Michael lived together. Is this the couch they shared? Did they pick it out together and split the money to buy it? Did Rory and Dean take up most of the space on it then, too? Did she fall asleep on Michael's chest on it like she falls asleep on mine?

I scan the compact apartment. Was that their dining table? Did he cook for her, or did she like to cook? Did they ever have a candlelight dinner, or were they a eat-pizza-on-the-couch couple? Am I eating off their plates and silverware? Did she buy new stuff when she could afford it, or could she not bear to throw out what they had shared?

I peek through her open bedroom door. There's a pile of clean laundry on top of her made bed. The ring in my hand triples in weight. Do I have sex with Michael's fiancée in the bed he used to share with her? Do I feel her and taste her and hear her moan in the same place he did? Do I start and end the day with her where he once had? Where he should now?

Is that fair to him?

I drop the ring on the mattress and dig through the heap of clothes. I'm not sure at first what I'm searching for, but I know when I find it. It's a UCLA T-shirt—thin, heather grey, soft from being worn and washed. It's a men's medium. Every night that Estlyn has slept in clothes, it's been in a T-shirt like this. I push clothes aside until I find four more like it, assorted colors and designs, all the same size.

Estlyn sleeps with Michael most nights, even when she's in bed with me.

How often does she think about him? Every day? Or do some days pass without him crossing her mind? Does she not want to think about him? Maybe that's why his picture isn't on any wall, why I still don't know what he looked like. Does she feel guilty the days she forgets to think about him, forgets to miss him? Or do those days not exist? Maybe the pain never stops. Maybe she wakes up with it every morning. Maybe it's what keeps her up at night.

Maybe the pain is worse when I'm here.

Does it hurt when I touch her? Does it hurt because my hands aren't his, because my kiss is different, because I can't make love to her like he did?

My eyes sink to the ring box in my hand. I flip it open to see the fifteen diamonds—one fat and fourteen tiny ones sparkling in the band. Estlyn deserves Michael. She got me.

Estlyn's key unlocks the deadbolt. I snap the box shut and bury it in the laundry I frantically rebuild into a messy mound. After the door slams shut, I hear her sigh and the thump of her messenger bag against the floor. She plods into the kitchen and opens the fridge.

I step out of the bedroom to see the half of her body not hidden by the refrigerator door. "Estlyn?"

The next thing I know, a water bottle flies at me. I flinch as it bounces off my forearms. When I drop my arm shield, Estlyn's hands rise to cover her nose and mouth. "Oh my God, sorry. I thought you were someone else."

"Someone who would be rendered defenseless by a disposable water bottle?"

She reaches into the fridge and chucks another one at me. I huddle to cover myself, but it hits me in the shoulder.

"What the hell?"

"Hurts, doesn't it?" She shuts the fridge, a third bottle in hand, and leans onto the counter the way she did that first night. Except this time, she's not playing a game, not being scary-sexy Estlyn. She looks as if she's halfway through a marathon and can't figure out how to get to the finish line.

"You okay?"

She ducks her head to her two fingertips to scratch her scalp—carefully, so she doesn't mess up the hair pulled back in a curly ponytail. "Fine. Just tired."

"Because you're supposed to be on leave and you're too stubborn to take one?"

Without raising her head, she flips me off.

I chuckle, then lean on the opposite side of the counter. My thumb and finger hook under her chin. I don't tilt her face to mine. I don't have time to before she covers my hand with hers and presses her lips against my fingers. Her warm breath sends chills over my skin.

Her eyes, like black diamonds, glance up to mine. "Linus?"

I nod.

"What's your sister's name?"

"Leo."

"Leo?"

"Eleonor. But my mom liked to call us Linus and Leo when we were kids."

"God, your parents were mean."

Our breaths collide with each of our soft laughs.

"If Leo were in trouble—say, held hostage—and the kidnappers said they would set her free if you complied with their demands, would you?"

Why does this feel like some kind of lawyer trap? No, why do so many conversations with Estlyn feel like a trap? "Yeah."

"Suppose they wanted you to do something illegal. Would you?"

"Can I go to the police in this hypothetical?"

"No."

"Why not?"

"Because there's a warrant out for your sister's arrest."

"Why? What did she do?"

"She's innocent."

"Then wouldn't a trial prove her—"

She shakes her head. "You're overthinking this. Would you do something illegal to ransom your sister?"

"Yeah, of course. She's my sister."

"Would you steal?"

"Sure."

"Would you assault someone?"

"Is the person I'm going to assault evil or something?"

"No. He's an unwilling participant."

"How badly would I have to assault him?"

"How badly do you want to free your little sister?"

I stare Estlyn's eyes down as I weigh my options. "I mean, I would have to assault him, right? Because she's innocent too, and she could get killed if I don't. And my loyalty lies with my sister, not him."

"Why does your loyalty lie with your sister?"

"Because she's my family."

"But it doesn't lie with your dad, does it?"

I pray I'm never on the witness stand with her questioning me. "No, I guess it doesn't."

"So, you wouldn't assault someone to rescue your dad?"

"No."

"Why not?"

"Because he probably had it coming."

She tilts her head before she challenges me. "So it's based on merit—your loyalty?"

"Where are you going with this?"

"Would you kill someone to ransom your sister?"

What the fuck? That's where we've been going? "Why are you asking me this?"

Her tone sharpens as she straightens up and slaps the back of her hand against her palm. "A life for a life. Would you kill him to get back your sister?"

"Who is he?"

"A stranger."

It's frightening how desperate she is for my answer. Is this happening to her? Holy shit, is that why she had to go back to *work* so soon? "Estlyn, is Rory okay?"

Scoffing, she pushes off the counter. "Yeah, everyone's okay." She takes a swig of her water, then rests her hips back against the counter on the other side of the kitchen.

"Est?"

Nodding, she grips the lip of the granite behind her.

"Wanna get the hell out of here?"

"Yeah," she scoffs, "ever been to Dubai?"

Dubai? Okay, what the hell is wrong?

I go to the fridge, then pull out a bottle of Chardonnay. She sighs when I hand her the glass I poured. "Go sit on the couch while I pack."

"I can pack my own clothes."

I want to scream, *No, you really can't!* But that might give away the fact that the ring is in her laundry. Oh, or the fact that I was snooping around in her laundry.

"Where are we going?"

"A place not nearly as hot as Dubai."

TWENTY-FOUR

Estlyn

Six Days Prior

There's a difference between waking up to the purr of the ocean hundreds of feet below my window, with a highway and horns and morning joggers polluting the sound, and opening my eyes to the water so close the onshore breeze mists the window with salty spray.

That's all I pay attention to, the waves churning the sand. I curl around the down comforter and rub my thumb against the cool sheet and stare. I stare out the window at the sand that has swept onto the floor through the open door. I stare for a minute. Maybe several. Maybe an hour. Each wave counts the time, but I'm not counting the waves.

It's calming, this roar. A lullaby of something so powerful and peaceful and deadly. It's a mass grave, and no one seems to resent it for the lives it takes. Because it's not personal. It's just nature. It's the circle of life or some bullshit like that.

If only I were the ocean.

Linus stirs behind me, rolling onto his side to face the ocean like I am, but he doesn't wake. If he had, he would have slid his hand over my abdomen and pulled my back into his chest like he always does.

He brought me here last night, to this 1920's cottage in Santa Barbara. He told me it belongs to his grandparents, that he played in the water outside it when he was a kid. He told me he came out here right after he caught Erin cheating on him, after he lost his job. He told me he comes out here to write when he needs inspiration.

He told me he thought I could use some inspiration.

No shit.

I scoot toward the headboard to grab my glass of water from the nightstand. Before I can take a sip, I see the E. E. Cummings lines Linus left for me in the middle of the night:

You are tired,
(I think)
Of the always puzzle of living and doing;
And so am I.
Come with me, then,
And we'll leave it far and far away—
(Only you and I, understand!)
You have played,
(I think)

If She Plays His Game

And broke the toys you were fondest of,
And are a little tired now;
Tired of things that break, and—
Just tired.
So am I.
But I come with a dream in my eyes tonight,
And knock with a rose at the hopeless gate of your heart—
Open to me!
For I will show you the places
Nobody knows,
And, if you like,
The perfect places of Sleep.

That sappy bastard has a poem for everything.

The piece of paper is arched, like it's resting on top of something. I pull the poem back to find a box beneath it.

A ring box.

Holy motherfucking motherfucker. Shit, goddamn. Fuck, fuck, fuck! What the hell is *that*? No, really, what the fucking hell is that? Is Linus proposing? I don't know this guy. And he sure as hell doesn't know me.

Kids, this is why you don't have one-night stands.

What do I do? Do I open it? Do I just tell him no before I see the ring he picked out for me? Do I pretend I didn't see it?

"Morning," Linus stretches his sleepy voice

behind me.

Okay, so feigning ignorance is out. But I can't look at him until I have a plan.

"What do you want to do for breakfast?" His fingers zigzag down my arm until they lace through mine.

I don't roll over. I don't answer. I still don't have any fucking clue what to do.

"Est?"

"No, Linus."

"Okay, we don't have to get breakfast."

"No." I roll onto my back and look up at his face, propped in his hand. "No, I can't marry you. Are you insane? We just started dating. On a *trial* basis. I know we were moving fast but..." My eyes narrow at the most confusing expression he could give me. "Why are you smiling?"

"You found the box."

"And I'm rejecting you. So why—"

He smirks. "Open it."

"Linus, I'm sorry—"

"Open the box, dumbass."

Fine. I grab the box and snap it open.

My lungs stop.

My pulse stops.

The ocean stops.

It's not the same one. Can't be. It's just a remake, right? That'd be weird, though. No, that'd be impossible. Linus wouldn't know what it looked like.

I take it out of the box and slip it on my finger. My thumb twists it in a full circle to test its weight. My fingers flex and extend. I hold it out to glisten in the sunlight dispersed by the clouds outside.

It's Michael's.

I can't look at Linus when I sputter, "How did you— Are you— Are you going to get in trouble for this?"

"No," he says, a smile in his voice. "It's all yours. No strings attached."

No strings attached. The words I used the first night I brought him home. Words I no longer want to apply to us.

I swallow through the tightening of my throat, my gaze glued to the ring on my hand. "How?"

He lets out a soft chuckle. "Estlyn, come on. Didn't you tell me it's never 'just how it is?'"

"Did you have to pay for—

He answers by parting my lips with his. Heat rushes through my mouth and down my body. I grasp at his hair and dig my fingertips into the muscles that tighten along his spine, begging him to press his weight on top of me. I can't let his lips leave mine because if they do he might open his eyes. He might see that I'm crying.

But they do. They steal my air as his tongue tastes the goosebumps rising on my neck. When he presses up to pull my shirt over my head, he sees the tears sliding toward my ears. His smile is soft when his thumb swipes one away. The other tear he stoops to catch with his lips.

"Dillon," he whispers.

My eyes unleash a flood at the sound of my real name—the name of the girl Michael loved. The one his ring was for.

"Being with me doesn't mean you love Michael less." Linus slips Michael's shirt up my waist. "I'll never ask you to clear him out of your life to make room for me." Once there's no space between our naked chests, he brushes my curls away from my face. "I just want whatever room that's left."

I taste the warmth of his mouth and stroke his jaw before his hands sink mine into the mattress. Linus tastes different than Michael. His stubble is rougher. His hair is silkier. He's an inch taller. The skin on his shoulders isn't as smooth. His chest is broader, the muscles of his abdomen more apparent.

He's not Michael. He never will be.

But Michael sure as hell would have liked him.

I shiver under Linus, shutting my eyes to feel him on top of me, entangled with me, surrounding me, until my lungs release the words, "You can have it."

His hands leave mine, one pressing my thigh to the bed. His green eyes search mine when he says, "Thank you." They don't break my gaze as he pushes inside me. My toes curl in the sheets as he fills me. His fingers dig into my hips. My spine flexes away from the mattress.

Our sharp breaths mix, our sweat mingles, and then our voices collide.

I unwind beneath him afterwards, taking in the scent of his neck as it pulses with each breath he takes. My left hand lazy in his dishwater hair, I see Michael's ring. Not in Michael's hair.

I curve around Linus and clear my throat to thwart the tears. "Waffles," I whisper. "With chocolate chips and whipped cream and bacon."

"And coffee," he sighs.

He straightens his arms to roll off me. I flatten him back to my chest. "Not yet."

TWENTY-FIVE

Cal

SIX DAYS PRIOR

ESTLYN'S HAND SWINGS IN mine as we walk to breakfast. Her thumb slides along my finger. Her other hand holds my arm, the metal of Michael's ring against my skin.

Whatever fight she was losing yesterday, she's kicking its ass today.

Her arms are around my waist in line outside the cafe. She leans me against the yellow stucco as we wait. Her cheek against my shirt, I feel her voice on my chest when she says, "Why didn't you and Erin get married?"

"What?"

"You were together five years. Why didn't you ever ask her?"

"Who said I didn't?"

Her chin tilts up, resting on my chest. "You asked?"

I can't tell if she's jealous or relieved or indifferent about my answer. I'm leaning toward indifferent. She's not the jealous type or the kind to crave commitment.

Or is she?

What was Dean saying about her being fiercely loyal? Didn't he say she has her tribe or—no, her pack, and that she'd kill or go to prison for any one of those handful of people? Everyone else is a potential means to an end, but never those people. Is she trying to figure out if I qualify as someone she should *bend the world* for?

"We talked about it," I answer. "Erin said if we got married she'd be 'just my wife,' and I would put my career before hers so she'd never get to be a real actress."

"Is that how you treated her?"

Yeah, this is some kind of test. My answer will be graded. I glare down at her. "I lost my job after I got her a role on the show I worked on."

She lifts her hands defensively. "Okay. Sorry I asked."

I grab her hands and wrap them back around me. "We moved in together as a compromise."

"Which I'm assuming you didn't know included her fucking your father."

"Correct. Why do you ask?"

She shrugs and hugs me tighter. "I don't like men whose balls are smaller than mine."

Yep. I was right. It was a test, and I think I got a solid B. But who the hell really knows without a report card? "I don't think you have to worry about attracting that type of guy," I say. Resting my lips in her hair before—strictly out of curiosity, of course—I ask, "Would you ever get married?"

She shrugs. "Not until my dad can walk me down the aisle."

"When will that be?"

"Hopefully soon."

"You guys don't know?"

"It's complicated."

Weird. I thought prison sentences had a set end date, and then inmates tried to get out earlier for prison overcrowding or good behavior or whatever else their lawyers could come up with. But I don't have incarcerated family, so I wouldn't know what's normal.

"Speaking of which." I clear my throat. "I mean, not actually. On a completely unrelated note,"—I wave my hand to gesture—"one far, *far* away from marriage, which is not on my mind or in my plans,"—*Are you going to interrupt me, or do I have to just keep rambling until the words finally form a comprehensible sentence?*—"Do you—"

"Estlyn, party of two," the host calls.

Oh, thank God. I need to try that again.

After the host seats us and leaves our table, Estlyn says, "It was my mom."

"What?"

"That's what you were asking, right? Who my

dad killed?"

"I'm sorry, what?" *What?*

"Oh." Her hands slip around her coffee mug. "What were you saying outside?"

I lean over the table toward her. "That's why you were in foster care? Because your dad killed your mom?"

Estlyn brushes me off. "Bitch was in the middle of raping me. He pushed her off me, and she smacked her head and…" She makes a breathy *zip* noise as she slices the air in front of her throat.

How can she be so cavalier about this? What the fuck is wrong with her?

"He's in prison for murder two, but it was justifiable homicide. That's why we were able to appeal for a second trial. But you know, white moms in the jury and all. Bishop tried to weed them out, but the fucking DDA—"

I slap my hands on the table and shut my eyes. "*What?*"

There's a pause as she sips her coffee. "Was something I said unclear?"

No. It was clear. That's the problem.

Estlyn was raped.

Estlyn was raped by her mom. By her mom?

Estlyn's dad killed her mom.

Estlyn saw her dad kill her mom.

Estlyn went from rape victim to orphan in a handful of seconds—orphan because her dad tried to rescue her?

"How old were you again? Eleven?"

She nods and brings the mug to her lips again.

"Holy shit," I mutter and run my hand over my mouth. I've been having sex with an assault survivor? Why didn't she tell me? What if I've been hurting her or reminding her of what happened?

Wait, she likes being with me, right? She's not faking it and actually shutting everything out, is she? Or maybe she physically can't feel it at all. Can't that happen sometimes? Oh God, she's faking everything. She's afraid, isn't she? She feels pinned down when I'm on top of her. What about when I hold her hands against the mattress? What about that one time—

"You look whiter than usual. You okay?"

My fingers catch my jaw, then run up to the sides of my hair. I finally lift my gaze to her. "Have I—" I pinch my eyes with one hand. "God, I don't even—" Well, apparently, I can't speak at all this morning. I ease closer to her with my fingers spread to shield my face from half the restaurant. "Is sex...traumatic for you?" I whisper. "I mean, do you like— I just want to make sure I'm not—"

Her face is unreadable. A CIA analyst would get nothing looking at her. *Nothing*. So, I stop talking. I figure if I've steered this car toward a cliff, driving farther isn't going to save us.

"Linus, listen to me. I am not fragile. I am not breakable or broken. You will not treat me as such, understand?"

I swallow without saliva. "Yes."

"You will not look at or touch me differently. Because *that's* why I didn't tell you. I didn't know what it could be like before you, okay? So don't fuck that up."

Didn't know what it could be like before me? Holy shit, Estlyn likes me! Or maybe she's just using me for sex. Whatever, I'll take it.

"Okay," I answer because that seems more sensitive and light years more appropriate than doing that musical thing I wanted to do in my agent's office—stand on the chair, tip it over, and sing *I'm the best sex Estlyn's ever had!* I can do that later. In private. Where only I can witness the full extent of my douchiness.

My God, I'm going straight to hell.

I cover her hand with mine. "Estlyn, I'm sorry you went through—"

"Nope." She pulls her hand back and picks up the menu despite knowing what she wants already. "Try again."

"I can't say I'm sorry?"

Her eyebrow arches when she looks up from the menu at me. "Did you do something wrong?"

"This feels like a trick question."

She smirks and rests her hand on the table. "What were you going to ask me earlier? Outside?"

"Oh." My fingers slip over hers. She lets them.

"I don't even remember," I lie.

She scoffs but plays along. "Okay."

My pen slashes through another paragraph of narration. I hate revising. I think Estlyn should be handling this narration-to-aside conversion. It was her idea, and I'd bet good money she planted the notion in Whitney's head.

A breeze picks up, blowing some sand from beyond my beach towel onto my script. I brush it off, then glance at Estlyn lying on her stomach on the shore beside me. A few hairs escape her ponytail and dance over her face resting on her crossed arms. The soft skin of her back glistens in the noon sun, unobstructed by bikini strings. I would wake her up to help me fix my screenplay, but Dean's words echo in my mind: *Never wake a sleeping toddler.*

"Did you put your two weeks in at the bar?" Estlyn mumbles.

I guess she's awake.

"Nope." I cross out another narration paragraph. Damn, how many of these did I include?

"Why not?"

"Because I need the money."

Her right eye squints open at me. "You sold your screenplay. You're a professional writer again."

My sigh rolls into sad laughter. "After taxes

and Whitney's cut, it's not as much as you might think."

"Do you have enough time to write if you're working at the bar?"

"It doesn't really matter."

"Why? Because you refuse to gamble on your talent?"

"No—"

"Is it because you think you're a bad bet or because you're a pussy?"

I toss a handful of sand onto her back. She flinches, then backhands my shoulder. "Because I can't sign a lease without proof of a steady income, which screenwriting isn't yet. So I have to stay at the bar."

"Then don't sign a lease."

"I can't squat at Elliot's apartment anymore. One of these days, the Health Department is going to come over in hazmat suits and declare it a hazardous waste site."

Her shoulders shrug toward her cheeks. "Stay with me."

"Like move in with you?"

"Why not?"

I roll onto my side and prop my head up with my fist. "Are you asking me to be your live-in boyfriend?" This is what I wanted to ask her earlier—what I need to know. What happens in a week? Do we end? Do we stay together? But I never imagined a scenario without my own place.

"Oh, don't get all girly about it. I just don't want to have to leave the house to get laid."

I smirk at her and sing-song, "You *like* me."

She shoves my chest until my back hits the towel beneath me. Her hand pinches the loose bikini ties at her spine as she climbs on top of me. Thighs around my hips, she guides my hand to hold her bathing suit together, then leans down to my face. Her fingers rake my hair back, and her lips hover just above my mouth. "I don't half-ass anything. If you're in my life, you're going to stay in it, so you might as well save some money on rent." I taste her tongue and her bottom lip before she whispers, "Take the week to decide." Estlyn slides off me and lies back on her towel, this time face up.

My gaze slips down her long neck to her slender waist and the soft curve of her hips, hardly covered by her bikini bottoms. She pulls her knees up, planting her feet in the sand.

"If I move in, can we take Dean's key away?"

"*Fuck* yeah."

TWENTY-SIX

Estlyn

Day Of

I HEAR A CRASH inside my apartment when I push the key in the lock. Not one that includes shattered glass or plates, just a thump that might include broken furniture. Maybe bones. Behind my door I find Linus on the floor between my living and dining area with one of my dining chairs also flat on its back. "Did you try alcohol for the first time?"

Linus chuckles and grabs the dining table to stand. "No, I uh—" His cheeks warm beneath his stubble when he finally turns my way. He studies my salon-smoothed hair, effortlessly falling around my shoulders and boobs. "Wow. You look beautiful."

I wink. "Don't act so surprised."

"Why are you so dolled up?"

"'Dolled up?' Are you a woman collecting social security?"

"Shut up," he says as he scoots the chair back

into the table.

"I have a gubernatorial campaign fundraiser in an hour at The Majestic Downtown." I slip my shoes off and slide my spaghetti straps down my torso to preserve my professionally done hair and makeup. I pass him on my way into the bedroom.

"Sounds very pretentious. Congratulations."

"Thank you. I just came back to put my dress on." From outside my closet, I call, "What are you doing tonight besides falling out of chairs?"

"Working on my screenplay."

I step into my black dress and carefully wiggle it over my hips. I'm always afraid the fabric will rip when I buy one of these flat-ass, white-girl dresses. It fits everything but my booty. If I go a size up, my sad boobs will be so deep beneath the surface a search and rescue team wouldn't be able to save them. So, for the sake of my Kate Hudson tits, I risk splitting a seam with my Sir Mix a Lot butt.

But *damn* if it isn't one healthy butt.

"Why don't you come with me?" I ask Linus once the dress is safely to my waist.

He crosses his arms and leans against the doorframe. "This seems like a tie kind of event. Do I need a tie?"

My arms through the short sleeves of my black dress, I turn my back to Linus so he can zip it. "I have a bowtie of Dean's you can borrow."

"Why do you have one of his bowties?"

I drop my hair over my shoulders and tug the short skirt down my thighs. "He left it here for wardrobe emergencies."

"Wardrobe emergencies?"

I shake my head. "God only knows."

TWENTY-SEVEN

Cal

Day Of

THE LINE IS LONG outside The Majestic Downtown, the century-old historical building in LA which has most recently been used for filming superhero movies and rap music videos. Either of those sounds more fun than a political fundraiser, but neither of those has Estlyn in a black dress so tight I know *for certain* she can't be wearing underwear. For that, I'll endure a lengthy line for an event I have no interest in.

We don't get in the line.

Estlyn leads me to a side entrance that is neither lit nor guarded. She knocks on the door with a particular rhythm—three taps, two taps, one. Dean swings the door open.

"Bitch, why is he here?"

Well, hello to you, too, jackass.

Estlyn pushes past Dean into the hallway. "Wyatt's here to keep me alive."

Oh. Wyatt. Not me.

"Would you rather I die?"

"Sort of. Oh, hey, Cal!"

Dean pulls me in for a hug, which we've never done before. The whiskey on his breath explains it. Although, I have to admit, this is one of the best hugs I've ever had.

"Welcome, welcome!" he says as he pulls away. "Might I suggest trying the Gruyère and Parmesan beignets while you're here? They are to die for."

"They're just fried butter and cheese," Estlyn calls back as she walks ahead of us down the hall.

He brushes invisible lint off my shoulders and says, "But they're fancy, so they won't make you fat."

I'm so confused. Dean and I are a few steps behind Estlyn when I whisper, "What are we doing here?"

"Estlyn's working. I'm avoiding my ex. You're eating fried cheese and enjoying the show."

Yes, I'm sure this political fundraiser will be the best entertainment I've witnessed all year. Estlyn pushes through the double kitchen doors ahead of us, and I turn back to Dean for answers. "Why are we going through the kitchen?"

"We weren't invited," Dean replies.

Well, now I *really* want to be here.

"Gino," Estlyn says to the small Italian man whose birth I approximate around the fall of the Roman Empire. She holds him by the shoulders and stoops to kiss each cheek of his. "Thanks for helping me out. I owe you."

"Oh, don't say another word about it. Just do me a favor. Try the Gruyère and—"

"I already told her," Dean says as he snatches a handful of cheese balls off a server's tray.

"Have you met my boyfriend, Cal? He loves your restaurant," she says with a wink in my direction.

Oh, *Gino*. I *do* love his restaurant. Estlyn went commando there, too.

We're shaking hands when a voice from behind me says, "Hey, sorry." I spin around to see the DDA Estlyn met with at the bar. Colton? Quinton? Quin?

"My father dragged me into a conversation about whether or not rape should be a capital offense. That was half an hour ago."

"Don't worry about it. We just got here." Estlyn shakes her head and pours herself a glass of wine.

Did she just find a bottle and a glass lying around? Does she have a sixth sense for alcohol when it's within a hundred-foot radius?

"What's the verdict?"

"One yay, three nays."

"Any women in this conversation?"

He rolls his eyes at me as if I'll stand behind his next statement.

"Feminists."

Jesus. I don't know why I ever worried about Estlyn liking him.

Estlyn rolls her eyes at me the same way. "Assholes."

Quin takes a step toward Estlyn and brushes his lips against her cheek. "You look sinful."

"Well, I am. What time is your speech?"

"Seven-thirty."

"Break a leg."

"There are a thousand cops in this city," Dean interrupts. "You had to use Wyatt?"

"Yep." She gulps the wine remaining in her glass. "All right, let's fuck some people up for political gain."

Quin chuckles. "How can you say you're not a prosecutor?"

"See ya at the table," Estlyn calls from over her shoulder as she and Quin leave the kitchen out the opposite exit.

"What do we do now?" I ask Dean.

"Open bar," he mutters through a mouth full of fried cheese.

For not being invited, we sure as hell are acting like we own the place.

"Here." Dean hands me two martinis, then grabs a pair of Old Fashioneds from the bar in the ballroom. "Can you carry any more, or should we make another trip?"

"I think four drinks are plenty for you to start."

"They're not *all* for me," he says before taking

off.

I follow Dean as he weaves through the crowd of women in gowns and men in tuxes. He stops at a table just in front of the stage. If we weren't invited, how do we have a table—*this* table? We take two of the five seats marked *Reserved*.

"Whose seats are we taking?" I ask.

"Ours." He sips an Old Fashioned, squinting at me as he swallows it. "Is that my bowtie?"

"Dean, right?" a brunette beside him asks. I'm guessing she's an event photographer, what with the dark pants and black V-neck—way too casual to be a guest. Oh, and with the camera hanging from her neck.

"Emory?" He grins and reaches his hand out to her. After they shake hands, he gives her a martini, then turns back to me with his finger raised. "That's my bowtie."

It's a basic, black bowtie. How can he tell?

"Estlyn said I could borrow it."

"It's there for emergencies."

I shrug. "I guess this was enough of an emergency."

He huffs and jabs his chest with his finger. "*My* emergencies."

"Well, I guess drinks on the house at the Dive are for *my* emergencies only."

His eyes narrow, and I hold his stare. "Looks good on you."

Wyatt sidles up to the table with Estlyn on

his arm just as an invisible emcee asks everyone to take their seats. All of us but Estlyn do. That's when I understand what Dean meant when he said we weren't invited. The couple approaching our table does not look pleased to see us there. More specifically, they're enraged at the sight of Estlyn lifting her martini to them, Gatsby style.

"If it isn't the future governor of California, DA Gavin Young," Estlyn announces as she invites him to shake her hand.

He takes it but mutters to the woman beside him, "Call security to escort—"

"Oh," Estlyn interjects, releasing his hand and waving him off. "I'm not sure you want to do that."

Jesus Christ, what did Estlyn invite me to?

"Is that a threat?"

She turns to Dean and says loud enough for us all to hear, "Why does everyone always ask me that? Obviously, it's a threat."

Young stabs the linen-draped table with his fingertip. Through a forced smile and gritted teeth, he says, "Give me one good reason I shouldn't have you dragged out of here."

"You'll find out in forty-five seconds."

"Excuse me?"

"Honestly, I'm disappointed. You had me dump my phone at the door before our last meeting, but you didn't check me for a wire? Sloppy."

His face hardens. "You're bluffing."

"I could be." She shrugs a shoulder toward her cheek. "I do lie a lot. You know, though, I'm getting so damn good at it that it's losing its thrill." She gestures by twirling her hands in the air. "So, I'm having to create these grander, more convoluted lies to make it challenging, to get that same rush. This could be one of those massive lies. Or it is possible that my cards are simply better than yours? All that to say—" She turns to Dean. "Has it been forty-five seconds yet?"

"Good evening, ladies and gentlemen!" the speakers boom from the sides of the stage. Everyone's attention turns to the man behind the podium, DDA Quin Something. Everyone's but Estlyn's. She's fixated on DA Young's reaction even as she takes her seat across the table from him.

"Thank you all for being here tonight," Quin continues. "I'm Deputy District Attorney Quinton Cunningham, and I have the privilege of introducing you to your next governor, Los Angeles County District Attorney Gavin Young."

The room erupts in conditional applause, as if they're waiting for a better reason than cheese balls and free booze to empty their wallets for the DA's campaign tonight.

"I hope you all have had a chance to try the Gruyère and Parmesan beignets."

I still haven't, actually. Dean ate all the ones on the tray before we left the kitchen, and now

I'm feeling cheated of the full political fundraiser-crashing experience.

"They are superb and, by the way, donated—along with all the food for this event—by Gino Moretti, owner of Moretti's in Santa Monica."

More obligatory applause. Estlyn *whoops*.

"As a Deputy District Attorney here in Los Angeles, I have had the tremendous honor of working directly with DA Young, so I can attest to the ways he has improved the lives of so many in our county—especially how he's made our community one of the safest in California.

"Young has bolstered funding to LA County's police departments, both city and sheriff, without taking a single one of your tax dollars. How? Simply by being tough on crime.

"Young crippled our opponents in the War on Drugs by seizing their assets and allocating those funds to our dedicated law enforcement. In Young's eight years as LA County's DA, he has taken twelve million dollars in drug money from the streets of southern California. These funds have allowed local police departments to purchase tactical equipment, patrol vehicles, and give themselves generous bonuses without costing the taxpayers a penny."

Huh. That sounds shady. Should Quin really be saying the police decide to pay themselves extra with drug money? Doesn't that make them—and DA Young—look sleazy? If I were the DA,

I wouldn't be flaunting that in my campaign. But maybe his voters don't care. Or maybe they condone it. Maybe they view him as a sort of legal-loophole-exploiting Robin Hood—steal from a druggie, give to a cop.

"In addition, each of these drug arrests resulted in federal Byrne grants—or War on Drugs money—given directly to our local government, directly to you.

"Now, of course, the challenge of relying on forfeited drug funds and Byrne grants," Quin goes on, "is that when our men and women in blue have done their job clearing the streets of heroin, meth, and ecstasy, those funds dry up. A decrease in drug use means fewer drug busts. Fewer drug busts means less drug money to seize and smaller Byrne grants for our local government.

"But DA Young is resourceful." Quin punctuates each adjective with his hand. "As well as committed and tenacious. Two years ago, when these funds were dwindling, LAPD officers arrested a key player in the La Familia Gaviria drug cartel. Just a fledgling presence in our county at the time, he made plea deal after plea deal with arrested LFG suppliers, keeping them out of prison and giving the cartel an opportunity to thrive in our community. With Young's help, La Familia Gaviria is now the sole supplier of heroin in three southern California counties."

Shit. What the hell did Estlyn invite me to? Free drinks and campaign sabotage?

Young's fist is clenched on the table, his arm tense as if the rest of his body is what's keeping him from bolting out of his seat. Estlyn pulls a burner phone from her clutch and types a text. A few moments later, Young reaches into the breast pocket of his coat and pulls out a similar low-tech phone. He flips it open, reads what I can only assume is her message, and glares up at her.

Quin keeps talking. "With a steady supply of drugs restored to our community, DA Young secured an increase in forfeiture and Byrne funds. Now our police are well equipped to handle the problem Young created and get record arrest stats in the process."

The crowd stirs. Murmuring begins. I turn to Estlyn beside me, but she doesn't flinch. Her eyes haven't left Young's. Young whispers to the woman he demanded call security earlier. She glances at her lap, likely at her phone.

"I know, I know," Quin defends. "It sounds like a conspiracy theory spun together by a delusional and ambitious underling seeking a promotion. You're not alone in that thought. The FBI said the same thing to me when I approached them. It turns out, though, we were able to find enough evidence to file charges against DA Young."

One hand around her martini glass, Estlyn's other points up at the stage behind her. "Wait for it…" she says.

"Ladies and gentlemen, please remain calm and cooperate with the FBI as they arrest DA Gavin Young."

"*There* it is," she says, her upraised finger stabbing the air above her head. With a serene smile, she tips her martini to her lips, relaxes back in her chair, and crosses her legs as the room spins into chaos around us.

A SWAT team twice the size of the one that infiltrated Estlyn's apartment descends upon the ballroom from every corner. Because the order to *remain calm* always produces the opposite effect, there are lots of screams and panicked gasps and a handful of expletives thrown around.

Our table mixes into the noise. Wyatt stands and flashes his badge, demanding Young raise his hands where he can see them. The photographer Dean gave a martini to snaps photos of the FBI twisting Young's wrists into cuffs. Wyatt escorts a huffing and eye-rolling Dean to the back of the room, apparently so the FBI doesn't think he is fleeing the scene. I catch a glimpse of them ascending the steps to the media booth.

In the eye of the hurricane shredding the room apart around us, Estlyn savors her drink. Or tries to. "God, I hate a dry martini," she says, scrunching her nose after another sip. Setting her glass on the table, she asks, "You hungry?"

"What?"

"You didn't get any dinner. Are you hungry?"

Looks like I've officially missed my chance at trying one of those cheese balls. "I guess."

"Gino said he was making us some to-go bags. We'll pick them up on our way out." Estlyn stands and inches her dress down her legs. She nods up at Dean and Wyatt returning to the table. "Got the video?"

Dean holds up a USB drive. "Yep."

Wyatt leads us out the way we entered, through the kitchen. It's only then that I notice Gino's crew is already cleaning up. He never planned an entrée.

Young didn't have a chance at making it to dinner.

We all pile into Wyatt's patrol car and swing by the front of the building to pick up Emory, who is capturing the magic of Young getting shoved into the back of an FBI SUV.

In the backseat, Estlyn leans forward to the netted metal separation behind Wyatt. "Could you drop everyone off at my place? Dean and Emory have to publish the story before someone else does."

When the car stops in front of Estlyn's building, Wyatt opens the back door for us. Estlyn climbs out of the front seat, then grabs me by the shirt. I taste the gin on her tongue when she kisses me. As we part, she breathes, "That's what I was lying to you about," and slides back into

Wyatt's car. "Oh," she adds, "there are some of those fried cheese things in there. They're for you. Don't let Dean eat them."

My lips slip into a grin. "How long will you be gone?"

She shrugs. "Couple of hours probably."

That should be plenty of time.

TWENTY-EIGHT

Estlyn

Day Of

"You have five minutes."

I nod and wrap my fingers around the door handle. Before I can twist it, Wyatt's hand covers mine.

"I can see you when you're in there."

"I know."

"And hear you."

"Yeah. I got it."

"And we're recording everything." He lowers his voice to add, "Don't incriminate yourself."

I look up at Wyatt's deep blues and smile at the concern in them. "Y'all would've gotten me by now, don't you think?" I wink, and he lets my hand go.

My back against the door, I swing it open to the stuffy interrogation room. "Good evening, Gavin."

"Excuse me, you can't be in here," his attorney with less-than-perfect teeth starts. "My client has invoked his right to counsel."

I smirk when I recognize the leathery perv in front of me. "Professor Roth?" I knew he looked familiar when I saw him pass the two-way mirror, but I didn't have time to get a good look at him until now.

My least favorite law school professor tilts his head to the right and squints at me. "Collins?" He stands to shake my hand, not neglecting to give my curves a lubricious once-over—hence his being my least favorite law professor. "What are you doing here?"

"I need a moment with Young."

"Absolutely not."

I pull out the chair opposite them and press my hands into the table. "What's your time cost these days? Six hundred? Seven?"

"Twelve."

I snicker at Young. "For that price, he better swallow."

My hands push off the table, and I kick my foot onto the chair. My fingers trail up my black hose to their lacy top encircling my thigh. There, I've stashed a wad of Franklins in the elastic with a clip. I drop all of them on the table, then repeat the semi-burlesque show with my other leg.

"That's two-thousand. You're my lawyer for the next five minutes. And as my counsel, I want you to get me every candy bar and pastry-like snack from the vending machines. Yes, candy pieces such as M&Ms or Skittles do count as a candy bar. Since we are crunched for time, make sure those little chocolate donuts are the highest priority."

"Are you kidding me? No."

"No?" I hop up onto the table, letting my legs dangle over the side closest to him. My finger trails lazily up his arm. "'Come on, baby, don't tease me. You don't really mean no, do you?'"

Roth catches my gaze and my allusion to the words he once said to me in law school. (Don't worry. I got out of his office before his hand got all the way under my skirt.) He holds my stare for a moment before caving. I don't get down from the table until he has gathered the cash and left the room.

"Lawyer to lawyer, I recommend you get a new one." Young opens his mouth to speak, but I push my finger to his lips. "Shh… Don't saying anything. You have the right to remain silent. Invoke it."

I hop down from the table and take the seat opposite him. "I'll be honest. I considered it—the whole staging two murders thing. The second I had my mind made up, I'd think of my dad. And Rory. And prison. But then I realized you dropped the charges against Rory and me. That meant I didn't have to beat a case in court. I just had to beat you. No DA, no charges, right? And, as promised, you announced that Monroe's embezzlement debacle was a department error at that press conference where you restored his reputation and pension and erectile function or whatever else. So, what leverage did you have over Rory and me?"

I rock my head side to side. "Money? I guess. You stole all of mine and even had DDA Ramirez—" I pause and turn to the two-way mirror. "Make sure you get this part—*hock the engagement ring from my late boyfriend.*" I turn back to face Young. "But," I spread the fingers of my left hand in front of my face, "my kickass new boyfriend got it back for me." I stare down at the ring sparkling in the cool light. "I asked him to move in with me. Do you think it's too soon?"

Young scowls.

"I don't think so, either. Life's short, right? You never know when you're going to get shot or be forced to stage a shooting.

"Anyway, we were talking about leverage." My fingernails drum on the table. "My dad. Okay," I take a deep breath, then let it out slowly before I can continue. "That one kept me wavering. But that was a promise you'd have to keep after the election, right? I'd have to gamble three lives on your word. That's a shitty bet.

"So, I could have walked away, right? Without my life savings, sure, but I'd make more money. But you're a fucking DA. You really do have more power over my puny little life than anyone else.

Am I wrong? It's okay to shake your head." I wink, but he doesn't budge. "You can charge me with whatever crime you want as long as you have a fleck of evidence that I might be guilty. You can pile those charges so high I disintegrate under the weight of them. Who's going to stop you? No one. Because you're the fucking DA. Because you put that heroin in my apartment, you could always charge me with possession or intent to sell or something real creative like distribution to a minor. Get me my first strike, huh?

"So, obviously, I had to ruin your life before you could ruin mine. It wasn't retaliation. It was preemptive self-defense."

I sit back with open arms and crossed legs. "Finding how to screw you wasn't even a challenge—you weren't exactly walking straight after being in bed with the cartel. Emerson was the attorney for all the suppliers?" I throw a hand up. "Really? Why the hell would you let me see you two together? I'm insulted you thought I was too stupid to pick up on that."

I fold my hands on the table, then shift my weight over them. "How much did the cartel pay you for each of those plea bargains?"

Young answers by grinding his teeth behind closed lips.

"Now, I know what you're thinking: 'Didn't she have a meeting with Xavier? Didn't I transfer a hundred thousand dollars to an account in his name after I saw the In-n-Out security footage verifying said meeting?'" My lips split into a grin as I nod. "Yeah."

TWENTY-NINE

Estlyn

SEVEN DAYS PRIOR

XAVIER DROPS BACK INTO the booth. "I'm listening."

"I decided the best course of action would be to just give you the money without making you die for it."

He shakes his head. "What? I mean, you know, sounds good, but—*what*?"

"You'll have to play along, okay?"

"With what?"

"For the next week, they'll be watching you."

"Who will be watching me?"

"You'll be safe—likely the safest you've ever been—because they're betting on you staying alive and out of trouble until they need you."

"Need me for what?"

I wave him off. "It doesn't matter because it's not something you're going to do. But I'm going to slide this envelope to you like we're being all shady and whatnot. You're going to peek in there right now and nod like I've just given you all the information you need about the people I'm paying you to knock off."

"What?"

"Open it. Look inside. Nod. Can you do that?"

He nods and follows directions. "What is this?"

"I ripped a couple pages off my boyfriend's screenplay."

His eyes cut through his furrowed brows. "That's not cool."

My shoulders shrug. "It was an old draft, and he used up all my printer paper. Do you have any questions for me?"

"How am I getting paid?"

"Jayden's GoFundMe. My tech guy will deposit about five hundred anonymous donations of varying amounts over the next week. It'll be a *miraculous windfall*," I say, using air quotes on the last two words.

He nods.

"Anything else?"

"I, uh…" He stares at the envelope and shakes his head. "No?"

"My number is in the envelope if you have any other questions." I stand and sling my bag over my shoulder. "Out of curiosity, are you an organ donor match for Jayden?"

Xavier shakes his head. "No. You think I haven't thought of that?"

My cheeks heat as I stammer, "No, no, of course. Of course you have."

THIRTY

Estlyn

Day Of

There's a knock on the mirror, my one-minute warning from Wyatt. "Now, the doctors that were supposed to die," I continue, "do you remember them? Dr. Wathen and Dr. Rush?"

Young continues to glare at me.

"It's fine. The FBI have the recording of our meeting in your campaign office in case you need your memory jogged." I toss my hair behind my shoulder. "You know what's so fun? If you were going to be tried in state court, that recording would be inadmissible, but because they're charging you with federal crimes, it's fair game."

His fist tightens and his jaw twitches.

"I know. I was excited about that one, too. Where was I?" I look up at the florescent lights on the ceiling and tap my fingers on the table. "Oh, the doctors. I didn't lie. They are from another case—the philanderous one. Now, of course, because I didn't kill them, I had to get justice for my client—who is married to Dr. Rush—sans a bullet to her husband's head. Curious as to how I did it?"

He glares.

I grin. "I knew you would be."

THIRTY-ONE

Estlyn

ONE DAY PRIOR

A CLIENT HAS NEVER given me wine before. Nor has one ever encouraged me to drink on the job. Until Emory. I'm trying to figure out a straight way to tell her that I'm in love with her and want her to have my babies.

Nothing comes to mind.

I'm mid-sip of chardonnay when the front door of the Rushes' Brentwood home opens, letting in the dusk heat before Dr. Rush shuts it. "Good evening, Miles."

Miles's feet lunge from the floor at the sight of me. He doesn't jump toward or away from anything, just straight up in the air as if something near the ceiling will protect him from me. "Who the fuck are you?"

I don't rise from my seat at his dining table, choosing instead to take another drink of my wine. "Mm… Emory has incredible taste, you know?" Swirling the wine around, I watch it stick to the sides of the glass. "She said you bought this bottle on your honeymoon in Napa. You were saving it for your twenty-fifth anniversary, right?"

"Who are you?"

I pick up the chilled bottle. "Did you want a glass?"

"No! I'm calling the cops."

"That's a good idea. While you're at it, could you do me a favor and tell them about all the Fentanyl you prescribed for Ms. Caroline Gray?"

"What? Who the fuck are you talking about?"

I sigh. "It was a pain in the ass to find dirt on you besides the whole you-being-a-whore thing. That'll destroy your marriage, but not your career. Your career, though," I point to him with my elbow on the table, "you'd be lost without that, wouldn't you? So, let's sit down and talk about how it's over." I pat the table near the seat kitty-corner from me.

"I have no idea what you're talking about. Get the hell out of my house!"

"Do you supervise a resident named Joseph Nguyen?"

His teeth grit. "Why?"

"Dr. Nguyen has prescribed Fentanyl patches to a patient named Caroline Gray for the last three years. Does this ring a bell?"

"No, I would never let one of my residents do that."

"But," I hold up Caroline Gray's prescription history, "you're technically the prescribing physician for the Fentanyl since you're Dr. Joe's attending. Therefore, you're responsible for whatever he does. Since he's an overworked surgical resident getting paid less than minimum wage, I think it's safe to assume his doctor's salary isn't paying for his oceanfront condo. Do you agree?"

Miles crosses his arms and shrugs. "How the hell should I know how he pays for anything?"

"You might want to learn since he made you an opiate supplier."

His fist pounds the table he still hasn't sat down at. "I'm not! I had no idea!"

I circle my fingers through the air. "I'm not sure this toddler defense is going to work on a jury, or on the chair of your department for that matter. Lucky for you, I have arranged a way for you to get out of this."

"Who are you? How the fuck did you get into my home?"

My God, he hasn't moved beyond that yet? "Funny you should ask. It's not your home anymore."

"Excuse me?"

"I have taken the liberty of drawing up your divorce papers."

"Divorce?"

"Shit," I whisper. "Did I forget to mention that? I thought it was obvious since I was breaking into your silver-anniversary wine fourteen years too early." I take another sip and clink the glass down onto the table. "Emory is filing for divorce. Now—"

"Why?"

"She knows about Reagan."

"Who?"

"The resident you're screwing. As I was saying—"

"I am *not* cheating on my wife! Who are you to accuse me of something like that? I don't even know you."

I let out a loud sigh, then dig through the file and pull out a stapled packet of text messages between Reagan and Miles. "Reagan sent you: 'Can't stop thinking about last night. Love how you bent me over my bed and fucked me from behind. My ass misses the feeling of you pushed against me. My pussy misses your dick.' You, being the gentleman you are, replied: 'My dick misses your pussy. Send me a pic.' Then she sends—" I flip the page around to show a picture I'm visibly uncomfortable holding. "So. The divorce papers."

He drops into the chair at the far end of the table and runs a hand back through his thick head of ebony hair. "Where's my wife?"

"Emory requires the house, full custody of the children, child support, and alimony."

He cackles. "Nice try. We have a prenup."

I nod. "Sure. You can go that route. But," I hold up Caroline Gray's file, "then you *will* get fired. How much do you have left in student loans?"

"I think I'll take my chances,"

I smile. "Great."

I hold my tablet up. His eyes narrow, then widen when he sees the email I drafted to his department chair with that sketchy patient file attached. My thumb hovers over the send symbol.

"Wait!"

I tilt my head, patient in the silence before his next words. They'll be my favorite of this meeting. Because the scales have tipped, and he finally knows they'll never go back in his favor.

"I'll sign it. She can have the house and the kids and the money."

I set the tablet on the table and slide the document his way with tabs highlighting the sections he needs to sign. His pen hurries over each line, scribbling his personal life into oblivion. When he pushes it back across to me, it's with such force I get a paper cut when I stop it from sliding off the table.

After finishing off my wine with a gulp, I stand. "Pleasure doing business with you, Dr. Rush. Emory will be home at noon tomorrow. She expects you and your belongings erased from her home before then. If you are still here, you will be escorted from the property."

"What about my kids?"

"They're with her parents for the night."

"I meant in the long run, you little bitch."

With my same pleasant tone, I respond, "You have visitation, the details of which you can iron out in court."

He fumes in silence as I pack my bag and let myself out. My hand on the doorknob, I lean back and add, "Oh, and make sure the dog is gone when you leave tomorrow."

When I get into my car, I send that email I drafted to Miles's boss with Caroline Gray's file attached.

THIRTY-TWO

Estlyn

Day Of

Young seethes silently in front of me.

"Oh, honey, don't feel bad," I say as I lean over the table toward him. "My cards were better than yours."

The interrogation room door opens behind me. Wyatt's hand is on the door handle while Professor Roth fumbles with a dozen and a half snacks cradled in his arms. The dumbass couldn't find a bag? Also, he actually bought the junk food I demanded? That makes me feel more badass than anything else tonight. He drops them on the table in front of me.

"They didn't have chocolate donuts, so I got you powdered donuts and a Ding Dong instead."

Yeah, like that's the same thing. I look up at Wyatt, standing in the doorway, shaking his head at me.

"Can I get a ride home?" I ask him. "And a grocery bag?"

I HEAR THAT SAME thumping sound from earlier when I unlock the door to my apartment, except this time it's followed by, *ohs* and *shits* and boozy laughter. Inside, Linus is pulling Dean off the floor. He appears to be in the same post-crash position Linus was in this afternoon, with one of my toppled dining room chairs on the floor next to him. Emory is reclining on the couch with a glass of wine. The entire place is in disarray. The coffee table is pushed into the dining room, vacating the living room rug for whatever they're doing. There are cardboard boxes stacked against the wall and on the dining table. I peer past them into the bedroom. There's a pile of clothes in hangers lying on my bed.

Linus's clothes.

"Hey, Estlyn's here!" Dean's words slosh out as he throws his arms open.

Linus straightens up, and his eyes settle on mine. His mouth curves into a slanted smile as I take in his life scattered all over my home. "How'd Elliot take it?" I ask.

"He said I'm an idiot for not learning from Erin."

"Sure." I nod. "What did you say?"

"That you didn't like old white guys with hairy asses, so my luck should be better this time around."

"If you want to gamble on that, I can offer you a quarter of the closet."

"Okay, but, you should know—"

"I refused to give up my key in this deal," Dean interrupts.

Linus shrugs. "We compromised on the fornication-noise cancelling-headphone plan."

He smiles at me as I walk to him, smiles until I'm close enough to envelop in his kiss. "We'll just have to be *really* loud then," I whisper against his lips.

"Look," Dean interrupts, "this is all very cute of you two to flaunt your sure-to-fade feelings for each other in front of us single people, but, Linus, it's your turn." Dean picks up the chair and plants it upright on the rug.

Linus tucks me against his side. "I think it's Emory's."

Emory drinks the last of her wine and stands from the couch. "Nope, I have sole custody of two children, so I have to be responsible and all that shit. Also go to my parents because my kids are going to wake me up in six hours demanding I feed them."

We exchange *thank yous* before she walks out the door.

"What are you taking a turn at?" I ask Linus.

"Linus is celebrating moving in with you by doing that musical-chair thing."

"You guys are playing musical chairs?"

"No. Nope." Linus shakes his head. "We're not playing anything."

"Estlyn, it's that thing where you stand like this." Dean steps up onto the upholstered dining chair, setting one foot on the top of the back. He leans his weight into the chair back, then squeals when it tips forward.

I catch the chair and steady it before he can fall again. "How many times have you guys tried this?"

"Once or twice—"

"At least five times each," Dean says over Linus.

"Have you landed ever?"

Linus rubs the back of his neck. "Define *landed*."

"Dean, this is going to hurt a lot worse in the morning when you're sober."

In a resolute whisper, he declares, "Then I'll never be sober."

I push Dean out of the way and grab Linus's hand as I step up onto the chair. "Your problem is that you're leaning back when you're supposed to be following the forward motion. That's why you keep falling, I assume, backward." I point my toe on the dark fabric covering the chair back. "It's like skateboarding. When you're going down the halfpipe, you have to lean into the gravity that's taking the chair to the ground." My weight shifts over my left foot until the chair balances on the back two legs. It tilts until it hits the floor, where I land on my feet.

The guys clap behind me.

After I turn and bow, I point at Dean. "Now, call an Uber. I'm going to have loud sex with my permanent boyfriend."

THIRTY-THREE

Cal

TWO DAYS PAST

"Est, that's the third dress you've tried on." I roll onto my stomach and push my fingers through my hair, watching as she slides another reject down her legs.

"And you've gotten to see me naked every time I've changed, so stop complaining."

"Haven't all these people seen you before? Like, *many times* before?"

She flips me off and pulls another dress from her three-quarters of the closet.

"I like the first one," I say for the eleventh time from where I'm lying on her bed.

Our bed.

"The blue one? It's not too revealing?"

Too revealing? Since when has she cared? "I might not be the best person to ask," I say with a smirk, but I want to take the words back as soon as they leave my mouth. I should have said, *No! It's perfect!* Because now she's trying on dress number four.

The grimace hasn't disappeared from my face when she spins to face me in it. "What? What's wrong with this one?"

"You don't look like you in that."

"What do you mean?"

"I don't know." I rub the stubble on my chin. "You look too…"

"White?"

"Like you're about to go to brunch at a country club."

"All right," she smoothes the dress in the mirror, "then this is the one."

"What? Why?"

She collects the dresses off the bed and clears a space on the closet rod for them. I snatch her wrist and pull her to me before she can hang them. Her chest rises and falls against mine when I take her dresses and drop them onto the mattress. Estlyn doesn't move as I step behind her and sweep her styled hair in front of her shoulder to start easing down the zipper. My fingertips follow the skin of her newly naked neck to her shoulder, taking the straps with them until they fall down each of her arms. I press my lips to the side of her throat before slipping the dress over her hips.

When I walk away, Estlyn runs her hand up her arm, covering her waist just below her strapless bra. I pick up the first dress, and she sighs and offers me her arms when I hold it out to her. It's navy blue, soft and thin, strapless but not sleeveless, falling loosely around her upper arms and chest to halfway down her thighs. I smooth her hair to cascade down her back like before. My hands trail down to both of hers until I can wiggle Michael's ring on her finger. She leans her forehead to my lips. "They don't deserve you," I whisper. "Don't become less than you are just so they can."

Estlyn fidgets the entire drive to Valencia, the suburban city a valley northeast of us. She watches the cars scoot by in the traffic out her window but doesn't say a word until we're on her childhood street.

"This it?" I ask as I slow my car in front of the stucco house with the oak tree out front.

"Yeah," she sighs.

I climb out of the car and open the back door to retrieve the peanut butter cookies we baked earlier. "Do they know we're here?"

She shakes her head and points at the container in my hands. "Peace offering." Then she points at me. "Stranger who they'll feel awkward yelling and/or talking about personal stuff around."

I snicker. "Glad I could help."

There's a piece of paper taped to Estlyn's parents' front door that reads, *Come on in!* I feel her slender fingers slip between mine before I open the door. Her hand grips me as if she's afraid of what will happen if she lets go.

No one is in the house when we step inside, but voices and laughter and the smell of carne asada float in from the backyard. The collage of picture frames on the vaulted foyer wall catches my eye. Estlyn's high school graduation photo. Rory's, too. A photo from Rory and Olivia's wedding. College graduation photos for each of them. Estlyn, Rory, and her adoptive parents on the beach years back.

Huh.

A picture of Estlyn and Mr. Hayes. The picture has to be before the Collinses adopted her. She's little, definitely younger than eleven—missing one-and-a-half top teeth, her curls escaping two frizzy braids. They must have wanted her to have her family on the wall, too.

"Let's go," Estlyn says and tugs on my hand.

"Wait. Is that Michael?" I point to the picture in the frame on the far left. It looks like a selfie taken at a basketball game. They're in arena seats, both in Clippers jerseys. Michael flashes a goofy smile at the camera. Estlyn plants a kiss on his cheek.

They're perfect.

I look back at Estlyn. Shit. Her eyes are glassy.

"I don't like looking at pictures of him."

"Why not?" I whisper.

"Because he's not supposed to be twenty-two

anymore. But he doesn't get any older than that in photos."

I caress her cheek with my thumb, then cup her face in my hands. My lips press to her forehead, and then I whisper, "Introduce me to the rest of your family."

Estlyn leads me to the backyard, where a small crowd is scattered on the outdoor couches and picnic table under the patio covering. Everyone is chattering until the first person notices us. From the family photos, I deduce it's her mom. She nudges her husband's arm. He freezes at the grill. Mouth by mouth, the party silences.

For a long time.

Like, an eternity.

It hurts waiting for it to end.

So, I end it. I clear my throat and hold up the Tupperware. "We brought peanut butter cookies." I slide them onto the picnic table and back away like I've just lit a fire on the surface.

"This is Cal," Rory steps up with a light beer in his hand to introduce me. "He's the guy currently tolerating Dil. This is Dillon, who you all know, so don't be weird because this party isn't about her." Rory lifts his beer bottle. "It's about you all congratulating me for putting a baby in Liv."

There are gasps and ohs all around, and one, "Yeah, like it was a lot of work for you," from Olivia.

After all the usual questions of *when are you due?* and *how far along are you?* and the inappropriate one that someone always sneaks in, *were you trying or did you forget your pill?* I meet Estlyn's parents. Her mom holds back tears when she pulls Estlyn into an embrace. She hugs me, too, awkwardly rejecting my offer to shake her hand. Her mom asks about how we met and how long we've been together. Her dad shakes my hand and, at some point, asks if I like the Dodgers. I lie. But neither of her parents is very interested in us right now. It's Rory's night.

Oh, and Olivia's too, I guess.

THIRTY-FOUR

Gavin Young

FORTY DAYS PAST

THERE'S NO WAY ANYONE cleans these phones. I know the janitorial staff at my office didn't clean ours, so I made sure my assistant sanitized my keyboard and phone every week. But the black plastic of this handle is somehow both greasy and sticky when I lift it from the base. I restrain a grimace when I hold it to—but not against—my ear. My eyes meet the ones across the glass.

"Thanks for meeting me," I say into the receiver.

He scoffs, buzzing the line with the static of his breath.

"Look, Ted, I'll make this quick. The undercover operation that inadvertently incriminated you for embezzlement of LAPD funds?"

He nods.

"While I can neither confirm nor deny that—"

"It was bullshit."

I pause to measure my next words, my next

gestures carefully. I'm being watched. I'm being eavesdropped on. I'm on trial. Everything I say here is admissible in court. "Dillon Collins, formerly Dillon Hayes. She also goes by Estlyn Collins."

"Michael Bishop's girlfriend. I'm familiar with the little cunt."

"Because of the explanation we gave the public, she can't be tried in criminal court. But if you want to pursue a civil case, you can."

He scoffs at the word *civil*.

"Or…" I take a breath and glance up at the security camera. "If you want to try to catch her in an illegal act so they can file criminal charges, she's behind an organization called After Twelve. It's sort of a revenge—"

Officer Monroe ends the conversation with a deafening dial tone.

ABOUT THE AUTHOR

Growing up with poor reading comprehension, Laney Wylde avoided books at all costs. But after reading Francine River's Redeeming Love for the first time in high school, she fell in love with literature. It was then she realized broken anti-heroines and impossible love stories were the stuff of heart-wrenching, binge-worthy novels.

Afraid her slow reading pace and lack of writing skill would inhibit her from becoming a successful English major, Laney pursued her B.S. in Mathematics from Biola University, graduating in 2014.

Laney gathered the courage to write honestly and diligently in 2017, producing Never Touched, a passion project that sheds light on the uphill battle that is healing from sexual abuse.

She lives in Southern California with her dashing husband and precocious little boy.

ACKNOWLEDGEMENTS

I WROTE THIS BOOK during a tumultuous point in my life. My family was strapped for resources, I had lost the part time job that we relied on to pay the bills before my royalties materialized, and, because of our financial situation, I had limited access to mental health treatment. Long story short, I overdosed before I finished writing If She Plays His Game.

So, these acknowledgments aren't for the people who helped me with my book. They are for those who helped me rise up and stay standing long enough to write it.

E, thank you for your enduring, unwavering, and defiant love.

My MoFos, Lizzie, Stacey, Sarah, and Whitney, thank you for tolerating a group chat where I voice my strangest thoughts. I'm spoiled by all the ways you prop up my inconsistent confidence. Stacey, thank you for Lioness. It's hard to describe just how much comfort he brought me. Sarah, thank you for answering my calls and sending me graphics in the middle of the night.

You four are incredible.

My family—Robin, Paul, Grandma Audi, Jenny, Tom, Mom, and Dad—it is impossible to overstate how much I needed the support you freely gave at the beginning of my career. Thank you!

And, God, this time last year I was writing Never Touched. Getting published was a pipe dream. May I not misuse this gift of a platform, no matter how small, You've entrusted to me.